A Note to Readers

While the Morgan and Dunlap families are fictional, the events they encounter are real. Enrico Caruso did in fact sing in the opera *Carmen* the night before the famous 1906 San Francisco earthquake. He survived the earthquake and made his way home to Italy as quickly as he could.

The 1906 earthquake measured about 7.8 on the Richter scale. Because of the intense fire, we will never know how many people were killed. The best estimates are that between 1,000 and 1,500 people lost their lives in the earthquake and fire. More than 300,000 people were left homeless.

As Mark and Holly discover during their days in San Francisco, Chinese Americans were hated. When the earthquake and fire totally destroyed Chinatown, many city leaders wanted to move Chinatown so that the valuable land it was built on would be available to other people. Because of pressure from the U.S. and Chinese governments and fears of losing overseas business, that idea was dropped. Soon Chinatown was being rebuilt on its original location.

✯ *The* ✯

SAN FRANCISCO EARTHQUAKE

Bonnie Hinman

BARBOUR
PUBLISHING, INC.
Uhrichsville, Ohio

To Bill, my husband and my Internet research expert.

© MCMXCVIII by Barbour Publishing, Inc.

ISBN 1-57748-393-6

Published by Barbour Publishing, Inc.
P.O. Box 719
Uhrichsville, Ohio 44683
http://www.barbourbooks.com

 Member of the
Evangelical Christian
Publishers Association

Printed in the United States of America.

Cover illustration by Peter Pagano.
Inside illustrations by Adam Wallenta.

CHAPTER 1
A Big Surprise

"Did she say married?" Mark turned to his younger sister Holly, who sat beside him at the big dining room table. Holly's mouth was a round circle of surprise. For once she was speechless.

Mark looked back at his mother at the other end of the table. His older sisters were hugging her and giggling. A knot started in Mark's stomach when he saw his older brother shaking hands with Mr. Wilkins. They were both laughing.

"Mother's marrying Mr. Wilkins."

Holly had found her voice, but it was high and squeaky. When Mark looked at his sister again, he couldn't tell if she was shocked or upset or just excited. "Why on earth is she doing that?" Mark asked softly even though he wanted to yell over the laughter from the other end of the table.

"I guess she loves him," Holly answered, and a grin slowly spread over her face. "It's so romantic."

"She loves him?" Mark's words came out louder and harsher than he intended.

Holly grabbed his arm. "Hush, they'll hear you."

Mark frowned and leaned closer to his sister. "How can she love him?" he hissed in her ear. "I thought she loved Father."

It was Holly's turn to frown. "Well, of course she loved Father, but he's been gone for a long time. I guess now she loves Mr. Wilkins, too."

Mark slumped back in his chair. "It hasn't been so long," he said quietly, almost to himself. "Only two and a half years."

Sometimes it did seem like a very long time since his father had died, but right now wasn't one of those times.

Mr. Wilkins had been a friend of their family ever since Mark could remember, and Mark had always liked him. He was a writer and traveled quite a bit doing research for articles and stories. When he came to visit, he told funny stories about his travels that made the whole family laugh. Now Mark felt like a traitor to his father for even liking Mr. Wilkins.

"Mark, Holly, come here," their mother called.

Holly jumped up from her chair and bounced toward their mother. Mark slowly got up and pushed his chair in until it rested neatly against the table. At last he had to raise his eyes and look at his mother. Her face was pink and young looking and filled with a huge smile. She looked happy.

"What do you think?" Mother said with a laugh as she hugged her two youngest children. "Your sisters said that they suspected something was in the works." She reached a hand out to touch Mr. Wilkins's arm as he moved to her side.

"I think I like the idea," Holly said and smiled shyly up at Mr. Wilkins.

"Mark?" Mother asked as she smoothed his hair.

Mark took a deep breath. He was shocked that his mother would even consider being married to anyone but Father, but he didn't say that because all he could see was her happy face. And Mark wanted his mother to be happy, so he forced his lips to turn up in a smile and reached out his hand to Mr. Wilkins. "Congratulations. Happy to have you." It wasn't a ringing endorsement of the marriage idea, but his mother seemed satisfied.

"We should toast the happy couple," Mark's twenty-one-year-old brother Peter said. With much laughter, they clinked milk glasses and coffee cups in a toast.

"Quiet, everyone, quiet," Mother shushed them all. "Let's have a prayer for our new family." Obediently the Morgan children circled around their mother and joined hands while first she and then Mr. Wilkins prayed for God's blessing on them all.

Mark found it impossible to concentrate on the words being said. But he was able to pray. "Please, God, help me." Those words ran through his head over and over long after Mr. Wilkins said amen.

Half an hour later Mark sat slumped on the front stairs. He could hear the rest of the family in the back parlor playing some game. A cheerful slightly off-key whistling signaled Peter's presence in the hall. It was too late to leave gracefully, so Mark just sat where he was.

"Hey, pal, why are you sitting out here alone?" Peter asked. "My team could use you. We're getting slaughtered in there." He yanked his head toward the parlor. "Mother and Christopher are on my team, and they're practically useless. They just keep looking at each other and smiling that goofy smile."

Mark made a face but didn't answer.

Peter sat down beside Mark. "Were you surprised about this wedding? Didn't you suspect it the same as Carol and Allyson and I did?"

Mark shrugged his shoulders but still didn't say anything.

"But now that you know all about it, everything should be fine. Just a little adjustment." Peter leaned back on the steps.

"How can you say that?" Mark jumped up and faced his brother. His face felt hot. "How can she marry him? Has she forgotten about Father?" Mark paced back and forth in front of the stairs. "I thought she loved Father, but maybe she didn't. And I never thought Mr. Wilkins would try to take Father's place."

"Whoa, boy, wait a minute," Peter said as he unfolded himself from the stairs. "You've got it all wrong."

Mark stopped pacing, folded his arms, and stared at Peter, waiting.

"Calm down and sit down," Peter ordered.

Reluctantly Mark did as asked, and the two of them sat down on the stairs again.

"Mother loved Father very much. It broke her heart when he died. You know that as well as I do." He waited until Mark nodded briefly. "But God intends that life goes on for those left behind when someone we love goes to heaven early. Mother and Christopher were lucky to find a way to make a new life together. Did you know that Christopher had a wife and son who died of cholera many years ago?"

Mark lifted his head. "No, I didn't know that."

"Well, now you do," Peter said and ruffled Mark's hair. "Everything is going to work out. Why don't you come help us beat the girls at that silly game?"

Mark nodded and watched his brother bound up the stairs two at a time before he started down the hall toward the parlor. He felt more mixed up than ever. He wanted to believe his brother, and maybe he did. At least the part about Mother loving Father. But he didn't understand why she wanted to marry Mr. Wilkins. Maybe he never would.

The next few weeks were full of ups and downs. The wedding was scheduled for February 24, and Mark's sisters, Carol and Allyson, were acting as if it were the occasion of the year. Instead of protesting the silliness, his normally sensible mother went along with most of his sisters' ideas.

Mark, on the other hand, felt distinctly out of sorts. He snapped at Holly over every little thing until she began avoiding him. He knew he was being grouchy, but he couldn't seem to stop.

One sunny Saturday morning in early February found him in Uncle Abe's carriage house, polishing the automobile. The snow had been too deep to take the car out for a couple weeks, but Mark wanted to keep it shined and ready to go when the streets were cleared of some of the big icy chunks of snow left behind by the horse-drawn snowplows. His uncle had taught him to drive last summer after Mark had begged for months. He loved cars with a passion that he usually kept for his fossil rock collection and his trumpet.

"Mark, you in here?" The door of the shed squeaked as it was pushed open, and a dark head appeared.

"Over here, Maureen," Mark called. Of all the people that Mark knew, both friends and family, his cousin Maureen understood him best, which was kind of funny, since she wasn't related to him by blood. Maureen had been adopted by Uncle Abe and Aunt Elise just about three years ago.

"What a shine," Maureen said and picked up another soft rag to help polish.

"She does look nice, doesn't she?" Mark stood back a moment to scan the car's fender. "Maybe we can all take her out tomorrow if the weather stays halfway decent and there isn't some other crazy wedding preparation to make."

"How's all that coming along?" Maureen asked.

Mark made a face. "Don't ask. They're all crazy." He stood up and flopped his rag up over his head in imitation of a woman's hat. "We just must have this lace on the dresses, and of course we want those fancy sandwiches, and do you suppose we could get hothouse flowers?" He made his voice high like his three sisters.

Maureen giggled. "That bad, huh?"

"Worse," Mark said in a mournful tone. "Of course, Carol and Allyson think they know everything there is to know about weddings, and Holly just wants to be sure that she gets a new dress."

"How about Mr. Wilkins?" Maureen asked. "What's he have to say about all of this?"

Mark sighed before answering. "He's underfoot all the time. He comes over almost every evening to see Mother and always wants to take the family somewhere."

"How does he act? Toward you, I mean."

Mark quit polishing again. "Oh, he's nice enough, but that doesn't mean I want him for a stepfather. I thought our family was doing just fine."

"Maybe your mother thought there should be a man in the house since Peter is gone so much."

"I'm practically a man myself," Mark said. "I can do most of the things that Peter does."

"That's true," Maureen agreed.

"In fact, I could probably handle everything, but now Mr. Wilkins will try to take charge."

The shed door rattled and burst open to reveal an out-of-breath Holly. Mark's sister was a little short for her age and a tiny bit plump. Her red face indicated that she had pressed her short legs to great speeds to bring her to Maureen's house.

"Mark, Maureen," she said between gasps. "Mr. Wilkins wants to take us to the theater this afternoon, to a vaudeville show. Mother is busy, and he asked the three of us specially."

Mark frowned. He'd love to go to a vaudeville show, but not with Mr. Wilkins.

"That sounds like fun, Holly," Maureen said, "but I'm afraid I can't go today. I promised Mrs. Figg that I'd help her open some crates of artifacts that arrived for the museum."

"I don't know," Mark said.

"Oh, go on, Mark," Maureen said. "It'll be fun. What can it hurt?"

"I should help you and Mrs. Figg." He and Maureen used to work for Mrs. Figg every day. She was a wealthy widow who had made her mansion into a museum. Now the pair only worked when there was a special project.

"Maybe later. If we need help with the crates, we'll just

work on something else today." Maureen folded up her rag.

Still he hesitated.

"Mark, please," Holly said. "He might not take me by myself. He might want to wait, and I really want to go today." Her brown curls bounced as she tugged at Mark's arm.

"Oh, all right," Mark said at last and allowed himself to be dragged off toward home.

An hour later they had eaten a quick lunch and bundled up for the trip to the Orpheum Theater. The trio caught the streetcar at the corner near the Morgan house. Mark was excited in spite of himself. He glanced at Holly, who looked like a bluebird in her blue wool coat with matching muff and hood. She chattered to Mr. Wilkins as they rode. Sometimes Mark envied his sister's easy way with people, but right now Holly was entirely too friendly with this intruder to their family.

They reached the Orpheum Theater with time to spare before the show was scheduled to begin. Mark had seen the inside of theaters before, but they always fascinated him anew. This one had thick carpets and intricately carved woodwork. The huge curtains screening the stage looked like plush red velvet. The seats were padded and comfortable but itchy if bare skin got against the horsehair covering.

"Have you ever seen a vaudeville show, Holly?" Mr. Wilkins asked as they settled into their seats a dozen rows from the front.

"Not a real one," she answered as she removed her coat and carefully spread it over her seat. "We went to a magician's show last summer, and once we went to some kind of wild animal act, but never to a true vaudeville show." She plopped down and gazed around her. "Peter promised to take me sometime, but he didn't get around to it yet."

"How about you?" Mr. Wilkins turned to Mark.

Mark nodded. "Once. Uncle Abe brought my friend Jens and me." Mark smiled as he remembered how they had laughed at the show. He and Jens had held their sides from laughing so much.

The next couple of hours passed like ten minutes for Mark as the comics joked and did impersonations. Ballet dancers pranced across the floor and two women sang, but Mark's favorite act was at the end. Two acrobats took the stage and performed twists in midair, cartwheels, and somersaults. What amazing strength and skill!

"Did you like the show?" Mr. Wilkins asked as soon as they were settled on the streetcar going home.

"Oh, yes," Mark replied. "It was something to see." The fast-paced show had kept him from thinking about his troubles all afternoon.

"I loved it," Holly said. "Thank you for taking us, Mr. Wilkins. We probably would have gotten old before Peter got around to it."

"I doubt that," Mr. Wilkins said and reached over to straighten Holly's hood. "By the way, we've got to do something about what you two are to call me. This 'Mr. Wilkins' just won't do. It makes me feel like I should act extremely dignified, and I can't keep that up for long." He frowned in concentration. "I'll have to speak to your mother."

The ride home was short as they talked about the show. Mark looked at his big house as they dashed up the front walk. Some of the electric lights were already on, giving the windows a warm, welcoming glow. It was home, and Mark relaxed. Maybe everything would work out.

"You're back," Mother called as they burst through the front door. She thrust her head out of the study doorway. "How was the show?" She swept out into the hall, wiping her hands on her big white work apron.

"It was wonderful." Holly twirled around and up to Mother. "You should have come. It was funny, and there were acrobats and singers and even ballet dancers." Holly attempted to demonstrate a step or two but slipped on the polished floor.

"Be careful," Mother said as she reached out to catch Holly before she could fall. "Did you like the show, too, Mark?"

"Yes," Mark said as he peered around the study door. Boxes sat on the floor, and the furniture had been moved. "What happened?"

"Oh, I'm cleaning and rearranging." Mother said and then smiled up at Mr. Wilkins. "Christopher will need a place to work—an office—and this seems like the best spot." She turned and waved a hand at the study. "I've packed up some things, but it turned out to be a bigger and dustier job than I thought."

"But," Mark said in a soft voice, "this is Father's study." Sometimes he slipped into the room just to feel close to his father. How could his mother even consider giving this room to a stranger?

"What's wrong?" Mother's smile faded. She put her arm gently on Mark's shoulder. The two of them moved farther into the room while Holly and Mr. Wilkins took off their coats and hung them in the hall closet.

Mark sighed and ducked his head so he didn't have to

face Mother's probing eyes. "I was thinking that I might move my collections into Father's study." He had thought of using the study but hadn't been quite ready to move Father's things, to make any changes in a room that held so many memories. Mark swallowed hard. Now it was being done for him.

"I'm sorry," Mother said. "I didn't know." She brushed his hair back with her hand as she often did.

"This is Father's study," Mark said more loudly this time.

"Yes, it was." She smiled and reached out to stroke the edge of the huge desk. "He loved it in here." She took a deep breath and straightened. "But he's gone now," she said firmly, "and I think he would want this room to be used."

Anger and despair fought within Mark. Maybe his father would want his study to be used, but not by an outsider. Mr. Wilkins was pushing his way into their lives and now their house. All the laughter and good feelings of the afternoon drained out of Mark. He wanted to escape, so without a word, he turned and ran. He spared only a glance at Holly, who frowned at him, but he clearly saw the worried look on Mr. Wilkins's face. He shoved past them. Good. Someone else should be worried. Maybe the man would change his mind. But Mark didn't really believe that was going to happen. He ran down the hall and toward the back door. Getting out was all he could concentrate on, even if it was only to sit on the step outside in the cold.

CHAPTER 2
Wedding Day

After awhile, Mark grew cold outside and took the back stairs up to his room. His mother didn't come up either to scold him or to say that she was wrong.

At dinner Mother announced that Christopher had decided to use a small storage room on the second floor for his office. No explanation was offered, and Mark certainly didn't ask why the plans had been changed.

"It's also been decided," Mother said, "that you children are to call Mr. Wilkins by his first name, Christopher. I told him that I thought that was disrespectful, but he insisted." A small smile crossed her face even as she shook her head in apparent disapproval. "He said that friends of any age should call each other by first names. And that's what he wants to be to you, a friend." Mother looked briefly at Mark and then picked up her fork again.

Mark kept his attention strictly on the plate in front of him. He felt happy that the study was to remain as it was, or at least he thought that was what he was feeling. Life was so complicated lately.

The next couple weeks sped by, and before Mark could get things figured out, the big day arrived. Saturday, February 24, dawned bright and sunny. There was a foot of snow on the ground, but two days of above freezing weather had cleared the streets.

"Mark, shouldn't you be getting dressed?" Allyson asked as she passed her brother in the upstairs hallway with an armload of clothes.

Mark looked down at his pants and shirt. "I am dressed." He wondered about his sister's eyesight.

"For the wedding. Surely you're not wearing that for the wedding." Allyson gave him a disgusted look.

"Well, maybe I will." He pretended to adjust his shirt and brush it off. "Besides, it's only ten o'clock. The wedding isn't until two o'clock—or at least that's what I've been told a thousand times in the last two weeks."

"Well, just don't wait too long," Allyson said.

Things were in an uproar downstairs. Carol was presiding over preparations for the late lunch to be held in their dining room after the wedding at church. Apparently some of the food was being delivered from a fancy restaurant and hadn't arrived on time. Carol was yelling into the telephone, which sat on a small table in the hallway by the front stairs. She hung up with a clatter just as Mark walked by.

"Terrible connection," she muttered. "That cake better

get here soon." She marked something on a piece of paper in her hand before she noticed Mark. "Isn't it time for you to get dressed?"

Mark threw up his hands. "It's only ten o'clock. It's too early." There was a rap on the front door, which, when opened, revealed people carrying armfuls of flowers swathed in brown paper while others carried boxes. They pushed past Mark, who pressed himself against the entryway wall to let them by.

Carol appeared and then Allyson and eventually Peter bounded down the stairs. Everyone talked at once, but soon the confusion subsided as the food went to the kitchen and the flowers to the parlor. Peter saw the last of the delivery people out the front door and shut the door with a bang.

"What a mess," he said to Mark with a smile. "Women and weddings." He gave Mark a closer look. "Say, Brother—"

"Don't say it," Mark interrupted Peter. "I know. Why am I not dressed? I give up." He shook his head. "I'm going to get dressed right now." Mark stomped up the stairs. The best thing he could do was stay out of the way of all this chaos. And get dressed of course.

Two o'clock came all too soon for Mark. He stood beside his brother at the front of the church with Christopher on Peter's other side. Mark had attended weddings before but had never been up front like this. It made him nervous to have so many people looking at him, even if they were all family and friends.

His mother was actually marrying someone besides his father. How could that be happening? His head told him that widows got remarried all the time, but his heart said something else. He gave a side glance toward Christopher, who looked nervous, too. In a moment Christopher's face relaxed and lit up with a big smile. Mark turned back and saw that his sisters were coming down the aisle. They were serving as bridesmaids. Mark would never admit it to his sisters, but they all looked as pretty as some of the pictures in Mrs. Figg's museum. Dressed in lacy yellow dresses, they looked like early spring flowers.

Then he saw his mother. She, too, was dressed in a lacy dress but it was a light tan color. Her brown hair was tucked up under a matching bit of lace. In spite of everything, Mark had thought that she might change her mind, might decide not to marry Christopher. One look at his mother's face put a stop to that notion. She glowed with happiness as she looked up the aisle at Christopher. There was no doubt of any kind written on that face. Mark took a deep breath. This was really going to happen. There was no stopping it now.

The wedding went smoothly, and soon they were back at home for the party. The house was filled to overflowing with people. Everyone told Mark how handsome he looked and how wonderful it was that his mother had married such a fine gentleman. Just when Mark thought he couldn't take one more pat on the head, he saw Maureen motioning to him from across the dining room.

"Hi, cousin," Maureen said with a grin. "I thought maybe you'd like to take a break from all these lovely festivities."

Mark groaned. "Would I ever."

"Let's go sit on the back stairs landing," Maureen said. "No one will notice us there."

In a few minutes they were tucked away out of sight, if not out of hearing of the celebration.

"I brought provisions," Maureen said and produced two

pieces of cake wrapped in linen napkins. Mark accepted his, and they nibbled in silence for a few moments.

"Everything seems to be going well," Maureen said.

"I suppose so," Mark agreed. "I can tell you one thing for sure. I'm never getting married if this is what you have to go through."

His cousin laughed. "I couldn't agree more." She wiped her fingers on the napkin's edge as she finished her cake. "I don't think all weddings are like this. My mother said that your mother intended to have a small ceremony, but Christopher wouldn't hear of it. He wanted the whole world to celebrate with them."

Mark raised his eyebrows. "I think the whole world is stuffed in our house right now."

"At least all of Minneapolis and half of St. Paul," Maureen said. She took Mark's napkin and folded it up with hers. "Do you feel any better about this marriage?"

Mark leaned forward to trace the curve of the stair railing with his finger. "It's done with. I have to live here, so I'll have to get used to him living here, too. I don't like it, but what can I do?" He shrugged his shoulders. "But he's not my new father, no matter what those people down there say. I don't need a new father."

Maureen just nodded.

An hour later the festivities were winding down. Mother and Christopher changed clothes so they could go to the train station to leave for a short honeymoon trip south to Mankato. Peter had to go back to college the next day, but the rest of the children would stay at home under Carol's supervision. Mother and Christopher would be back on Thursday.

Uncle Abe planned to drive the newlyweds to the train

station in his big car. Some of the others would be following along in cars and carriages to wave the couple off.

Mark went out on the front porch. His uncle's car shone in the late afternoon sunshine. Mark and Maureen had polished it for hours to get it looking so fine.

At last Mother emerged with Christopher behind her. In a few moments they were settled comfortably in the back seat of the car with a blanket wrapped around them. Mark watched as other party goers hurried off to load up as well.

Uncle Abe opened the front car door and then stopped. He turned around and called, "Mark, why don't you come and do the honors."

"What do you mean?" Mark ran down the sidewalk.

"Come and drive your mother and Christopher to the station," Uncle Abe said. "I'll just go along for the ride."

"Are you sure?" Mark stopped beside his uncle. He had driven this car many times before, but never with any passengers other than Uncle Abe or Maureen.

"I'm positive. Hop in. I'll crank." Uncle Abe went around to the front of the car and cranked until the engine sputtered to life. Mark climbed in the driver's seat and adjusted the choke until the car was purring smoothly. As soon as Uncle Abe was settled in the passenger's front seat, Mark put the car in gear and eased away from the curb and into the street. He relaxed as much as he had at any time in this long day. Driving a car always made him feel in control and almost powerful. It was something he could do well, and he knew it.

Uncle Abe was talking to Mother and Christopher as they drove along. Mark kept the auto at a slow speed because he knew that his mother was still a little nervous about vehicles that didn't have a horse pulling them.

"This is a fine automobile you have here, Abe," Christopher said. "I've often thought of getting one myself."

Mark perked up his ears. This was the first good news he'd heard in days. Christopher was interested in automobiles. Perhaps he might buy one. Mark's fondest dream was to have an auto. Until he could accomplish that on his own, the next best thing would be for Christopher to buy one, wouldn't it? He frowned to himself. He didn't want to owe his stepfather a favor, that's for sure.

"There's only one problem," Christopher yelled over the noise of the motor. "I've traveled around the world and done all sorts of dangerous and exciting things, but I don't have any aptitude for driving an automobile. I can't buy an auto unless I show a little more promise as a driver."

Mark frowned again. That figured. Just when there was a glimmer of better days to come, Christopher dashed it. Mark shook his head. In doing so he caught a glimpse of movement to his left. After that everything happened fast.

The movement was a horse Mark hadn't noticed before. Reins dragging, it appeared to have been spooked by something. Maybe the backfire of a car behind them had startled the animal. It happened all the time. He seemed bent on running right in front of Uncle Abe's car. Mark slammed on the brakes and swerved. The car slid sideways into a small ditch and stopped with a jolt. The horse brushed the fender of the car but ran on unharmed.

Mark just sat for a moment. Then he turned to see that his mother's hat had fallen forward over her eyes. She seemed fine otherwise.

"Are you all right, boy?" Uncle Abe asked. The motor

had stopped, so his uncle's voice sounded loud.

"I'm fine." Mark looked at his uncle. "I'm sorry. I should have seen that horse sooner."

"Don't know that anyone could have. Fool horse anyway." Uncle Abe swung his door open. "Let's see what we can do to get this machine back on the road. Time's a-wasting."

By this time others had driven up. "Are you hurt?" Peter yelled as he waded the muddy ditch to come up beside them. His face was white.

"We're just fine," Mother spoke up for the first time, "but we're going to miss our train if we don't get going."

In a few minutes the car was pushed out of the mud, cranked up, and off down the road once more. This time Uncle Abe was driving. Mark had just shook his head when Uncle Abe offered him the steering wheel again. This was not the way he wanted to show off his driving skills. He wanted to be thought of as an adult, not a kid who ran the auto in the ditch. Not much chance of that today.

By the time the newlyweds had been waved off at the station, Mark was more than ready to head home. All he wanted was to get in bed and cover up his head. *Please, God,* he would pray, *don't send any more days like this.*

CHAPTER 3
Another Surprise

The house seemed awfully quiet to Mark after all the festivities were over, and even Holly was subdued for a day or so. On Monday everyone had to go to school, including Carol, who was a teacher, and Allyson, who was attending normal school studying to become a teacher.

Stella was left at home alone to clean and do the huge washing left behind from the party. Mark heard her humming as he raced out the door to school, so he supposed that she was glad to have the house to herself. He missed his mother, although he wouldn't admit that to anyone. The day dragged on. It didn't help that the weather had turned disgustingly damp and gray.

At last Mark was free to go home. His trumpet case

banged against his legs as he hurried through the mist that acted like it was going to turn to snow. He was anxious to get his trumpet out and try to play a piece that Mr. Schoggen, the band director, had given him. The band was playing for eighth grade commencement in May, and there was a trumpet solo in one of the numbers. Mr. Schoggen had asked him to try out for the solo.

Mark was excited to be asked because there were a couple of eighth grade trumpet players who were pretty good. His friend Jens, who played the clarinet, had just laughed when Mark asked him why he didn't try out for a solo, too. Jens was kind of shy, but Mark thought he played the clarinet beautifully.

Mark flung open the front door at home and almost plowed into a pile of boxes and suitcases and a big trunk that were sitting in the entryway. "What's all this?" he said to anyone who might be listening.

Holly's head popped out from behind the trunk. "It's Christopher's things. They weren't supposed to be delivered until after he and Mother got back from their trip, but the delivery men got the orders mixed up."

"What are we supposed to do with all this junk? It sure is in the way here." Mark hadn't thought about Christopher having things other than clothes that would now belong here in their house. He still couldn't bring himself to acknowledge that this was now Christopher's house.

"Stella says that you and I are to carry the small ones up to Mother's room and Christopher's new office. They're labeled," Holly said around the cookie she was munching on.

"I have things to do now," Mark said. "I need to practice my trumpet." He frowned at his sister.

"It won't take long," Holly said. "We're supposed to leave the big boxes and the trunk here."

Mark dropped his book bag and trumpet case with a clatter and began to pull off his coat and hat. "Seems like he could tend to his own stuff," he muttered, not really intending that anyone should hear.

"What did you say?" Holly asked. She took one last bite of cookie and dusted her hands together.

"Nothing," Mark said crossly.

"I don't know what in the world is the matter with you, Mark Morgan!" Holly planted herself in front of her brother, arms crossed and foot tapping. "You're like an old bear that got woke up early from his winter's nap. I suppose it's something to do with Christopher. You used to like him, and I don't know why you've changed your mind, but I'll tell you one thing. Don't spoil this for the rest of us."

Holly's voice dropped. "I like Christopher, and I like the idea of having a father around again."

"He's not our father," Mark burst out.

"Well, I should think I know that," Holly said, "but he'll act like one, and that's what I care about."

Mark just looked at his sister. Her brown curls practically quivered with indignation. She had put her finger on the one thing that was bothering Mark. Unlike her, he didn't want someone acting like his father. Someone telling him what he could do and more likely telling him what he couldn't do. He didn't need that anymore. He was old enough to make his own choices.

Mark picked up the nearest box. "Oh, all right. Let's get to work."

Holly's faced relaxed into a smile. "Yes, let's."

The week passed quickly, and Mother and Christopher returned on Thursday evening. Everyone went to meet them at the station and crowded into a big wagon for the chilly ride home. Mother was hugging everyone, while Christopher just smiled. Mark was so glad to see his mother that he didn't even care that Christopher was there, too.

The next couple weeks found the new family settling into a routine. Christopher got his things put away and finished setting up his office in the storage room. Soon he was back at work researching and interviewing and writing articles. Sometimes at supper he told about his work or his past travels. Mark listened to the stories with interest. He really hadn't understood what Christopher did until now. It sounded like fun and sometimes exciting, too.

One Tuesday toward the end of March, Mark slogged home from school through knee-high fresh snow. He had his afternoon all planned. First he was going to practice his trumpet because he had been picked for the solo, and then he was going with Maureen over to Mrs. Figg's house. Mrs. Figg had called last evening to say that she had some fossil rocks for his collection. He couldn't wait to see what she had come up with. He would have gone there directly after school if Maureen hadn't had to go home first to help her mother with a meeting.

At least this way he could get his practice out of the way. He pulled his desk chair over by the bed and propped the music there with a book. Soon he was working hard as he struggled to get the notes to come out just right.

"Mark, Mark." It took a moment or two before he realized that his mother was calling his name.

"Yes," he yelled and put his trumpet down.

Mother opened the door and came in. "Mark, could you practice some other time? Christopher has a tight deadline for an article he's working on and really needs some quiet to concentrate."

"But I need to practice my solo."

"I know, dear, and it's sounding quite good, but Christopher will be done in an hour or so. You could practice then." Mother straightened the covers on his bed and turned to smile at him. "Please."

"I guess so," Mark said. Maybe Maureen would be ready to go to Mrs. Figg's by now anyhow. He opened up his trumpet case and put his instrument away. He'd clean it later after he finished practicing.

Mother had gone out the door but stuck her head back in. "Would you please run some things to the post office for Christopher? They really need to get sent in this evening's post." She smiled apologetically. "More deadlines. Writers always have deadlines."

"Couldn't Holly do it?" Mark frowned. Nothing was going right this afternoon.

"The snow is kind of deep for her short legs." Mother stood in the door again. "If you can't go, I'll run them to the post office myself."

"No, I'll go." Mark pounded down the stairs to grab his coat and hat. Mother followed and picked up two large envelopes from the telephone table in the front hall.

"Here you go." She handed the envelopes to Mark. "Be careful now. Thank you."

The cold air felt good on Mark's hot face. Why couldn't Christopher tend to his own mail? And why did he suddenly need so much quiet to work? Mark stomped through the snow

28

until he felt better. Lately he felt aggravated more often than not, and it wasn't a feeling he liked.

Mother, Christopher, Holly, and Mark were the only ones home for supper that night. Allyson had a meeting at her school, and Carol was eating with Edward, her beau, at his parents' home. Mark was still feeling out of sorts, even though he did manage to get to Maureen's house in time to go see Mrs. Figg for a little while.

As usual Holly could make up for any silence on his part with her chattering. She was giggling before they even got the blessing done. Mother had to tell her to please be quiet so they could pray.

"Say, Polly, what happened to those envelopes on the hall table?" Christopher asked as he passed the chicken and dumplings. "I was going to run them to the post office after supper."

"Mark took them to the post office for you," Mother said.

Mark ducked his head to hide the surprise he felt. So it hadn't been Christopher's idea.

"Thank you, Mark," Christopher said. "You saved me a cold walk tonight. I heard you practicing your trumpet solo this afternoon. It's sounding great. I guess that's why you stopped sooner than usual." He passed the rolls to Mother.

Mark couldn't stop himself from looking at his mother, who had picked up a roll to butter it.

"I asked him to practice later so you could concentrate better, dear. With that deadline tomorrow, I knew you needed to work hard."

"You'll spoil me, Polly. Actually Mark's music doesn't

bother me at all. I've written in lots noisier places. Like when I was in Brazil during the carnival celebration." Christopher raised his hands over his head and pretended to sway to music.

"Tell us, tell us," Holly begged. "What's carnival?"

Just then the telephone rang in the hallway. Eventually Mark heard Stella answer. Meanwhile Christopher launched into a story about the carnival celebration in Rio de Janeiro, Brazil. Mark tried to listen to Stella with one ear and Christopher with the other, which wasn't easy.

"Mr. Wilkins, telephone." Stella said from the dining room doorway. "I told him you were at dinner, but he said it was important."

"No problem." Christopher pushed his chair back. "I'll just be a moment, darling."

Mark rolled his eyes but was careful not to let his mother see. Now it was darling. He poked at his dumplings. So Christopher hadn't complained about his trumpet. It wasn't right to stay annoyed with someone when the reason vanished, but knowing that just made Mark feel more irritated than ever.

Christopher was gone from the table a lot longer than a moment. Holly babbled happily, but Mark saw that Mother kept glancing at the door into the hall.

Finally Christopher came back and sat down. The others looked at him expectantly.

"Well," Mother said at last. "What was that about? Or was it a private matter?"

"Oh, no," Christopher said quickly. "I'm just taken by surprise."

"Surprise?" Mother asked. "What do you mean?"

"That was the managing editor over at the newspaper, the *Chronicle*. The paper wants me to go to San Francisco. They want a series of travel articles about San Francisco and points in between."

"How wonderful," Mother said. "Will you be gone a long time?"

"There's more," Christopher said and reached over to take Mother's hand. "He wants the emphasis to be on family travel, so he suggested that I take you along."

"Me, go to San Francisco?" She looked at Christopher and shook her head. "I couldn't be gone so long. I wouldn't want to leave the children. But it does sound wonderful. My cousin Judith and her family live out there. I'd love to visit them, but no, it would be too long to be away."

"Actually, Holly and Mark could come with us, and the girls could manage fine alone."

Mark and Holly stared at each other in shock.

"We couldn't possibly afford such a trip," Mother stated firmly and picked up her fork. "And that's that. Although it's a lovely idea, Christopher."

"The expenses would be paid by the paper," Christopher said. "As part of the family travel angle."

Mark saw Mother swallow hard.

"Be that as it may, they can't miss so much school. Why I imagine it would require two or three weeks at least."

Holly started to say something, but Mark shook his head slightly, and for once she paid attention to him and closed her mouth.

"Probably at least two weeks and maybe a bit more," Christopher said. "It takes several days to get there on the train."

"It's out of the question," Mother said. "They're bright children, but three weeks is too long."

"I agree," Christopher said.

Mark's heart sank, and he saw Holly's smile disappear.

"Or I would agree, ordinarily," Christopher continued.

Mark and Holly traded looks once again.

"But in this case I think it would be extremely educational for them to undertake such a trip. Think of all they could learn from what they saw. Besides, you said they were bright. Surely they could keep up with their schoolwork with our help."

"I don't know," Mother said doubtfully. "I'm sure it would be wonderfully educational, but it would be for so long."

Mark judged that it was time to speak up. "Mother, I think we could keep up."

"Of course we could," Holly jumped up and went around to hug Mother's neck. "We're smart. Please, oh please, let us go along. It would be so much fun."

"And very educational," Mark put in quickly.

Mother made a face. "I'm just not sure."

"It's totally up to you, darling," Christopher said, "but I think it would be a fine family trip."

Mother looked at each of them for a moment and then at her plate. "Oh, all right. We'll go. If the school agrees that you can make up your work."

This last statement was drowned in a chorus of cheers led by Holly. Immediately she began asking questions about the trip and offering opinions. Soon Mother was laughing along with Christopher and Holly.

Mark sat back down in his chair. Today had been full of

surprises. First Christopher had been complaining about noise and wanting Mark to run his errands. Then the opposite was true, and now this. Mark hardly knew what to think. So he decided not to think anymore. Instead he would just enjoy the adventure ahead. Surely a cross-country train trip would be a very big adventure, even if it did involve a stepfather.

CHAPTER 4
All Aboard

Mother voiced second thoughts about the trip every day for the next few weeks. It was short notice for such a big trip she said. Who would look after Carol and Allyson? How could she not be home when Peter came from college for Easter break? And really, it was not right to miss so much school.

To Holly's delight and Mark's secret relief, Christopher found answers to all of Mother's questions and concerns. There was plenty of time to make all necessary arrangements he said. Carol and Allyson could look after themselves with an assist from Stella. Peter would understand,

and Holly and Mark's teachers thought it was a great opportunity.

The day to leave was set for Saturday, April 7. Christopher said that would get them to San Francisco on Thursday, April 12. Mother telephoned her cousin Judith, who responded with excitement and an invitation for them to stay at the Dunlap house in San Francisco. Mark had never met his cousins since Judith and her husband, Albert, had moved to San Francisco many years ago. About all he knew was that Cousin Judith had three children still living at home who were near his age.

Departure day was sunny and only a little chilly with a few patches of snow left in shady places. The travelers and assorted family members gathered at the train station. Uncle Abe helped Christopher with the baggage while Mother said good-bye several times to Allyson and Carol and Aunt Elise.

"Bon voyage," Maureen said as she handed a package each to Holly and Mark.

"What's this?" Holly asked as she shook her package.

"It's a going-away present."

Holly and Mark tore off the wrappings to find Brownie cameras.

"Wow! Thank you," Mark said. He looked through the viewfinder.

"My very own camera," Holly said and grabbed Maureen around the neck. "This is great. Thank you."

"You shouldn't have," Mother said and shook her head at her brother and sister-in-law. "But it's a wonderful gift for a big adventure. Thank you."

"Just be sure that you record each and every bit of the trip," Uncle Abe instructed.

Maureen handed Mark a small bag. "Here's some extra film and the directions."

"I wish you were coming along, too," Mark said as he took the bag from Maureen.

"So do I, but someone has to keep an eye on things in Minneapolis. I can't wait to hear all about everything when you get home."

"I'll send you postcards." For a moment Mark felt homesick before he set foot on the train. He was going a long way from all that was familiar.

"All aboard," the conductor called from the train steps. With a flurry of hugs and good-byes, the family boarded the train and found seats. They were traveling by sleeper coach southwest to Omaha, where they would switch trains and start west the next morning.

Holly and Mark pushed up to the window to wave at the others on the station platform. In a few minutes the train slowly began to move. Mark waved one last time and sat down to get settled for the trip. Holly pressed her nose against the glass long after the station was left behind.

"Well, that's that," Holly announced. "We're on our way. How much farther until we get there?"

Mark groaned, but Christopher laughed. "Let's see. Only hundreds and hundreds and hundreds of miles to go. We'll be there before you know it."

It wasn't quite that fast, but the miles did slip away. They ate lunch in the diner car with its snowy white table-cloths and uniformed waiters. Mark spent most of the after-noon just watching out the window as they made their way through Minnesota. The train stopped frequently to let pas-sengers off and take on others.

"This train has stopped four times in an hour," he said to Christopher late in the day. "We won't get to San Francisco before May at this rate."

"You're right," Christopher said. "Thank goodness our train west from Omaha is an express. It will still stop some, but not this much."

Supper meant another trip to the dining car and an opportunity to look at the other passengers. Mark glanced around now and then while they waited for their steaks to be cooked. Uncle Abe had told him that the best fun on a train trip was seeing the other travelers. So far there didn't seem to be much out of the ordinary, unless he counted the lady with an enormous hat who could be heard loudly complaining to the waiter about some aspect of the service. Mark's sympathies were with the waiter.

Holly poked Mark and nodded her head in the direction of the woman. "She's a grouch."

Mark nodded and turned a bit to get a better look at the woman in question. She was probably close to Mrs. Figg's age and looked a little like his friend, but that was where the resemblance ended. Mrs. Figg was always polite and kind, and that certainly couldn't be said about this woman.

The steaks arrived, and Mark turned his attention to eating. It was good, but he felt like his stomach was swaying the opposite way from the train.

"Elbows off the table, Mark," Christopher said. "Here, let me show you a better way to cut that steak." He reached over and changed the way Mark held his knife.

Mark didn't say anything, but his face burned at being told how to eat in the midst of a crowded dining car. It didn't help that his stomach still swayed, so he ate quickly and asked to go back to the other car first. After Mother agreed, he made his way slowly between the tables. As he passed the hat lady, she leaned over to pick up something. The train gave a little jerk at the same time, causing Mark to bump into the woman.

"What is the meaning of this?" The woman's hat now sat at a rakish angle.

"Excuse me, ma'am," Mark began.

"I shall not be subjected to this abuse of my person." The woman's hat bobbed alarmingly until she reached up and jerked it back. "This train is full of ruffians."

"I'm sorry. The train jerked," Mark said. *And you leaned into the aisle,* he thought but didn't say.

"You, young man, are the worst of the lot." She did not acknowledge his apology and turned pointedly back to her food with a loud sniff.

Mark opened his mouth to protest her injustice but thought better of it when the train jerked again. Better to get away from her before he ended up sitting in her lap. Besides, he expected Christopher to appear any minute to see what other rules Mark was breaking. Good sense seemed to say that he'd better get back to his seat in the next car.

Mark was glad when the porters came through the train car later and began making up the sleeping berths. His stomach felt better, but it would be nice to lie down. He had heard about the berths or beds but couldn't visualize how they could come right out of the ceiling, so he stood as close as he could to watch.

The porter made it look simple. He flipped some levers, pulled on what looked like an ornately carved wooden shelf over their heads, shook out some curtains, and pulled the facing bottom seats together. Mark and Holly looked at each other in amazement when the porter produced two beds, one on top of the other, in less than five minutes. The finishing touch was a small net hammock that swung over each bed for holding belongings.

"It's like a little room," Holly pronounced as she stuck her head through the curtains into the upper berth.

"Like bunks with curtains," Mark said. Before long the whole car had been transformed in the same way. Mark and Holly were to share the top berth while Christopher and Mother took the lower one. They took turns changing into nightclothes, and for a few minutes all four crowded into Mother and Christopher's berth for prayers.

Finally Holly and Mark climbed on a step stool and into their berth. A small electric light lit the space dimly as they stowed their shoes and clothes in the net hammock.

"Pretty handy gadget," Mark said and stuffed his jacket on top.

"I'm not sleepy yet," Holly said.

"Well I am, so be quiet," Mark replied. The swaying wasn't bothering his stomach anymore. It might even make for pleasant sleeping. He reached over and switched off the light.

"Do you think we'll meet any cowboys or Indians?" Holly asked in the dark.

"I don't know," Mark said. "Probably, I guess. Lots of them live out west."

"Do they take trains?"

"I suppose so," Mark replied. "If they want to get anywhere fast, they would."

There was a knocking sound from below and the muffled

voice of their mother telling them to go to sleep.

"Good night," Holly whispered.

In spite of feeling tired, Mark lay on his back, thinking for a while. Soon Holly's steady breathing told him that she was sound asleep. The clickety-clack of the wheels was the only sound other than an occasional snore from someone in the berth across the aisle. Mark thought about how much his life had changed in the last couple months. Since Christmas he had gained a stepfather, and now he was on a train speeding through the night. Once in awhile the train swerved slightly as it rounded a curve, but mostly it rocked gently. Mark had finally drifted off to sleep when a sharper curve with a jerk rolled him up against Holly. Before he could get settled again, a shriek echoed through the train car.

Mark sat up and bumped his head on the ceiling above. What in the world?

"What was that?" Holly demanded in a sleepy voice.

"I don't know." Mark scrambled over Holly to peer out the curtain opening. Holly shoved her brother over and joined him.

There was some kind of commotion several berths down. The car lights were low, so it was hard to see what was going on at first. Then a porter switched on more lights just as other heads poked out through their berth curtains. A woman continued to yell, although the shrieks subsided to outraged shouts.

"What's going on?" Mark asked Christopher, who was looking out from below.

"I think that frightened gentleman you see must have fallen into the lady's berth when we went around that last curve."

Mark craned his neck and saw a young man sitting on the floor while the yelling woman gestured at the conductor and then at the downed gentleman. The woman looked a little familiar.

"That's the hat lady!" Mark exclaimed. "That man fell into the hat lady's berth."

"Poor fellow," Holly said.

The hat lady was minus her hat now, but she wore a pink ruffled cap and matching wrapper. Her face was a darker shade of the same pink as she continued to shake her finger at the man who struggled to get up.

"I know how he feels," Mark said.

In a couple minutes, the conductor managed to get the gentleman on his feet and out the door. Still muttering, the hat lady disappeared back behind the curtains of her berth.

"Show's over," Mark said and pulled Holly back into their berth. There were no more shrieks, and soon they were both sound asleep.

The train had already arrived in Omaha, Nebraska, the next morning when Mother leaned into the upper berth to wake Holly and Mark. Quickly they dressed and gathered up their things. Their next train was scheduled to leave at 9:00 A.M., so that gave them a few hours to eat breakfast and stretch their legs.

It felt good to be back on solid ground once more. Mark felt stiff from the night spent in the small berth. He wondered how on earth Christopher, with his longer legs, could sleep at all in a berth. Maybe he was just used to it.

Their baggage sat in a pile on the platform, and Mark went over to ready it for the baggage handlers.

"I'll do that, Mark," Christopher said. "I want to be sure

the name tags are still there, and besides, some of these are too heavy for a growing boy like yourself."

"I'm strong," Mark protested, but Christopher had already hailed a porter, as if he thought Mark couldn't read a name tag or lift a puny suitcase. Mark turned away in disgust.

The family was ready to board the new train well before departure time. As they stood waiting on the platform, Mark looked around to see who else was there. Some of the other passengers might be going all the way to the West Coast, too.

"Mark, look," Holly ordered. "It's a cowboy." She pointed behind her.

Across the platform Mark saw a tall lanky man wearing a big hat and pointed toe boots. When he saw Mark looking his way, he smiled, which made his face crinkle into a thousand wrinkles. Mark couldn't help smiling back at the cowboy.

"I think you're right," Mark said to Holly.

"Do you suppose he's going on our train?" Holly asked.

"Maybe. We'll know soon enough. The conductor is putting the steps down."

"He's in the line," Holly said excitedly. "Maybe we'll get to meet him."

"Probably," Mark said. "He looks friendly."

There was a flurry of movement and sound off to one side. Mark swung around but couldn't see what was happening. The line continued to move slowly as the conductor checked tickets and directed the passengers to the correct cars. The crowd parted abruptly behind them, and Mark saw the cowboy sweep off his hat in a courtly bow and allow a woman to step ahead of him.

"It's the hat lady," Holly hissed. "She's on this train, too."

"I can see that. Maybe she'll be on a different car at least."
Mark wanted to groan. He didn't care to have another run-in
with that woman. He could hear her now as she evidently
gave the cowboy a piece of her mind about something. Mark
looked back one last time before stepping onto the train. The
cowboy was nodding politely as the hat lady talked. His eyes
met Mark's over the woman's head, and he winked before
turning his attention back to the hat lady.

Mark grinned as he followed Holly onto the train. This
leg of the journey promised to be interesting.

CHAPTER 5

Heading West

Mark forgot all about the cowboy and the hat lady when he saw his family's quarters on the train. The newspaper had arranged for them to travel west in a palace car.

Mark couldn't believe his eyes when he stepped inside. There was a narrow corridor with four doors spaced along the length of the train car. Christopher opened the second door to reveal a suite of three small rooms.

One center room opened into two even smaller ones on either side. They all had fancy curtains and plush velvet seats and carved wooden trim.

"Mark, look at this," Holly called from one of the side rooms. "It has a bathtub."

Sure enough, there sat a small bathtub near a wash basin and mirror.

"I wonder where the toilet is," Holly said with a frown.

"There's a ladies room at one end of the car and a men's at the other," Christopher said.

"Just like on the sleeper," Holly said.

"That's about all that's like the sleeper," Mark said, although he did see some fold-down berths similar to those on the sleeper.

"There are other special cars on this train," Christopher said. He stowed some of their baggage in a storage area in the corner. "There's a parlor car and a smoking car and an observation car. Of course there's a dining car and several sleeper cars, too."

The train whistle blew, and in a few minutes the train chugged out of the Omaha station. Holly and Mark explored every nook and cranny of the suite, and by the time they were finished, the landscape outside had changed from city to farmland.

A conductor stopped to let them know that church services would be conducted at ten o'clock in the parlor car.

"How wonderful," Mother said. "I thought we'd just have to miss services today."

"I almost forgot it was Sunday," Holly said.

"Sometimes I get my days mixed up when I travel," Christopher said. "Let's go."

"Not so fast," Mother said. "We may not have time to bathe, but we can certainly wash up."

Mark groaned. Maybe this fancy suite with a bathing area wasn't so great after all.

The parlor car was one car forward through an enclosed vestibule between the cars. It had velvet upholstered chairs and couches, and in the corner was a pump organ. The conductor sat at the organ playing "Rock of Ages" as several passengers drifted in.

Mother sat down in one of the velvet chairs and began singing along with the organ. In a few moments several of the other passengers sat on the chairs or on the couches. As it turned out, one of the sleeper car travelers was a minister going to visit his daughter in Laramie, Wyoming. The conductor had asked the Reverend Nichols to lead a short worship service.

The minister pulled out his Bible and read Proverbs 3:5-6. "Trust in the Lord with all thine heart; and lean not unto thine own understanding; in all thy ways acknowledge him, and he shall direct thy paths." He closed the Bible and looked at his small congregation.

"Trust is seldom an easy thing to do," the Reverend Nichols said. "Life is uncertain at best, and we human beings don't like that. We want to feel that we are in control, yet God says to trust in Him rather than trying to figure things out on our own. If we do this, He promises to help us in every way. Some of you are on your way to new lives, some are returning to old ones, and many are visitors. The one thing we have in common is a need for the blessings that God has promised right here in the Bible. Trust in the Lord, and He will direct your paths, no matter where the events of life may find you."

Mark watched the Nebraska farmland speed past outside while he listened to the minister. He knew firsthand how hard it was to trust in God sometimes or in other people. He had trusted his father to be around while he grew up, but it didn't happen. That wasn't his father's fault, but the fact remained that Mark and Holly and the others had only their mother now—and Christopher, if Mark wanted to count him.

Mark remembered his grandmother saying that God works in mysterious ways. God's ways had seemed mighty mysterious lately, but all the same he was trying to trust. He hoped that God understood how hard it was sometimes.

The minister spoke for a few minutes before closing with prayer and another song. While they sang with the organ, Mark noticed that the cowboy had slipped in at the end of the car. He had shed his coat to reveal a neat traveling suit. Mark judged the man to be older than his stepfather but younger than Mrs. Figg. His face looked like it had seen plenty of sun and wind, but perhaps he wasn't a cowboy after all. Cowboys were supposed to be wild and rough, and this man was obviously neither. How to meet him was the question.

Holly took care of that without the least hesitation. She walked up to the cowboy and said hi. After chatting with him for a few moments, Holly waved at Mark to join her.

"This is my brother, Mark, Mr. Wirts."

"How do you do, Mark? My name is Ian Rudolph Wirts, but my friends call me Rudy." He shook hands with Mark and once more his face crinkled into a million cracks when he smiled. "Fine service, wasn't it? I do enjoy some good hymn singing and a message to put your noggin to thinking."

"Rudy is a cowboy," Holly said. "He's been to Chicago, and now he's on his way to San Francisco to visit his sister, Bernetta."

"Yes, sir. This is my winter to travel." Rudy motioned for Holly and Mark to join him on one of the velvet couches. "I guess you could say that I'm hanging up my spurs, or at least the ones that kept me roaming all over Texas and

Wyoming herding those ornery cows."

"What are you going to do?" Mark asked.

"I've done done it. Bought myself a fine little spread in North Texas. Aim to raise horses."

"What about cows?" Holly asked. "You going to raise cows, too?"

"No, miss," Rudy said and shook his head. "The only way I want to look at another cow is when I'm forking up a nice juicy beefsteak."

"Why?" Mark and Holly asked at the same time.

The million-wrinkle smile returned. "I'm bound to say that cows are just purely trouble. You get one cow with a mind of his own, and he can get the whole herd riled up. No, cowboying has been good to me, but I'm going to raise horses now."

"You like horses?" Holly asked.

"Oh, yes. A horse is a noble beast of intelligence and good nature."

"Uncle Abe used to have a horse that kicked every time he tried to put the harness on." Mark could still remember his uncle mumbling to himself when Mabel kicked. "Uncle Abe got rid of her eventually."

"Too much inbreeding," Rudy said with a solemn nod. "It can cause fractiousness and a right mean streak."

"We'll just see about this. Where's the conductor?" A strident voice rose over the hum of conversation and the noise of the train wheels.

Mark didn't even have to turn his head to know that it was the hat lady, but he did look to see what was going on. Her hat was a different, smaller one now, but it, too, bobbed with indignation. It wasn't clear what was disturbing her, but the conductor was taking the brunt of her displeasure. Talk about fractious with a mean streak. Mark couldn't help thinking about mean old Mabel the horse. He wished they could get the hat lady moved to the country just like Uncle Abe had moved Mabel.

"Poor woman," Rudy said with a shake of his head. "Sorely in need of a spring tonic, I surmise."

Holly giggled at that, and Mark smiled. It was an interesting idea—a spring tonic to improve the hat lady's disposition. He had his doubts as to its effectiveness but didn't voice them. The hat lady followed the conductor out the door of the car, complaining all the way.

Mother and Christopher walked up before anything else could be said. Mark and Holly introduced Rudy, and Mother invited the cowboy to join the family for supper in the dining car. Rudy said he'd be there with bells on, which made Holly giggle again.

They ate box lunches at noon in their suite, and everyone settled down for the afternoon. Nebraska rolled past outside, and inside Holly and Mark did some reading at a small table under one of the windows. Mother read in one of the easy chairs, while Christopher unpacked his portable typewriter. The train stopped occasionally at this town or that, but mostly the rhythm of the wheels was unbroken.

Mark alternated staring out the window with reading his book. It was hard to concentrate, and the steady clacking of the train wheels made him a little sleepy. He glanced around the suite. It was nice to be here with Mother and Holly. Christopher was typing something at the small desk. At the moment it didn't even seem so bad to have Christopher here, either.

A little later Mark heard a soft snoring and looked up to see that Holly had fallen asleep with her head on her open book.

"Mark."

Mark looked to his left and saw Christopher motion from the door.

"What is it?" Mark asked when he reached his stepfather.

"Let's go to the smoking car," Christopher said softly. "I need to stretch my legs. Your mother and Holly won't miss us."

Mark saw that Mother was sound asleep, too, in her chair. Why not go with Christopher? He didn't have anything better to do. He was surprised that his stepfather had asked him to go somewhere without Mother or Holly since that hadn't happened before.

The smoking car was different in many ways from the parlor car. It had similar comfortable upholstered chairs, but in addition there were shelves of books in a tiny alcove and a barber shop tucked into one end. Mark saw a counter with glasses in a cupboard and several tables. Everywhere there were men smoking pipes or cigars or cigarettes. While they smoked, they read newspapers or talked as they sat around one of several tables. Some of them were playing cards, which surprised Mark since he didn't know anyone played cards on Sunday.

"This car is for men only," Christopher said. "The ladies can't abide the smoke. Can't say as I blame them."

"I guess you don't smoke?" Mark asked. He hadn't noticed before that Christopher never had a cigar or pipe in his hand.

"No. Never could stand tobacco. I can't see how swallowing smoke can be good for a person." He picked up a newspaper from a nearby table. "I'm going to catch up on the news. Why don't you look at the books? But be careful. You never know who you'll run into on a train."

"Be careful, be careful," Mark muttered to himself. "Always more directions."

While Mark looked through the books and magazines in the tiny library area, a nearby card game broke up. Three of the men walked off, but a fourth remained seated at the table. Mark moved closer as he pretended to gaze at the books on a shelf. The man at the table was slick from his heavily pomaded hair to his nicely shined shoes. He wore an expensive looking suit with a white shirt and had a gold watch fob hanging from his vest pocket.

The man was playing with a deck of cards. He was making the cards do all sorts of things that Mark didn't know cards could do. His hands moved quickly, and the cards appeared to walk from finger to finger and then to the table. There they were spread and seemed to turn by themselves and then back to the man's hands. Mark moved closer still to get a better view.

The man glanced up at Mark. "How do you do? Want a look at the cards?" He passed his palm over the cards, and they leaped to life.

Mark nodded. With an audience, the man's hands moved even faster as the cards leaped from hand to hand to table and back again.

"Let me show you some tricks," the man said and had Mark pick a card. He did several tricks and showed Mark how to do some of them. Finally the man showed Mark the proper way to shuffle the cards. "Have you ever played poker, my boy?"

"I doubt it," another voice said from behind Mark, "and

I further doubt that his mother would care for him to be learning at this particular time in his life even if it wasn't Sunday afternoon."

It was Christopher, of course, and Rudy was beside him.

"Up to your usual tricks, are you, Peterson?" the cowboy asked.

"Tricks is right. I was just showing the boy a few moves with the cards." The man smiled broadly at Rudy.

"Moves is the right word. But he doesn't need to know any of your moves," Rudy said.

"Let's go, Mark," Christopher said. His face was pleasant, but his voice was firm.

Mark frowned. He didn't need Christopher telling him who to talk to. He hadn't actually been playing cards—just watching.

"Come on, partner," Rudy said. "It's almost time for supper, and as you remember, your sweet mother invited me to eat with your family."

Mark hesitated but got up and pushed his chair in. Why bother to argue? His mother would just side with Christopher. Besides, supper was sounding pretty good. With a quick smile at the man, he walked away.

"So you met Lucky Larry Peterson," Rudy said as they went through the vestibule between cars.

"He didn't tell me his name," Mark replied. "Do you know him?" He still felt irritated with Christopher for butting in. Why couldn't he see that Mark didn't need someone to look after him?

"Everyone knows Lucky Larry," Rudy answered. "And many wish they didn't. He's a cardsharp. He can swindle the socks right off your feet."

Mark blinked at this bit of news. Halfway across Nebraska and already he had met a cowboy and a cardsharp. What would Monday bring?

CHAPTER 6
Stuck!

Mark expected Mother to lecture him about talking to a cardsharp, but the next morning came, and she still hadn't mentioned it. Evidently Christopher didn't tell her about Lucky Larry. Mark was glad, but at the same time he felt irritated that Christopher was protecting him from Mother's wrath. He could take care of himself without Christopher's help.

Monday morning they rolled into Wyoming. Trees and snowcapped mountains loomed to the west. By noon, blowing snow swirled outside the windows. The Reverend Nichols climbed down in Laramie to be greeted by his daughter and several grandchildren, who alternately climbed his legs and tugged him across the platform.

Inside the train, Mark and Holly worked at their school-work when they weren't arguing. Mark thought Holly complained too much, and Holly thought Mark was a grouch. Finally Mother took Holly off to the parlor car and left Mark to stare out the window at the snow.

The train slowed and stopped at a small town. Mark wrote out two or three math problems before noticing that, unlike at previous stops, the train didn't start up again in a few minutes. He wasn't sure how much time had passed before he realized that they weren't moving yet. He peered out the window. What was the problem? The snow had slowed, but the wind whipped the powdery substance into little eddies that whirled on the ground by the tracks.

Christopher pushed open the suite door. Behind him stood Mother and Holly.

"Why are we stopped so long?" Mark asked.

"This snowstorm dumped several feet of snow in the mountains ahead of us," Christopher answered.

"So we're stuck," Holly said with a big grin. "Isn't it exciting? We're snowbound." She bounced over to the window to look out.

"Not exactly snowbound," Christopher said. "Just delayed a few hours while we wait for the snowplow engine to come through."

"The conductor said it might be evening before the plow can clear the tracks," Mother said. "I hope this won't make our train late getting into Oakland. I don't want Judith and Albert to have to wait for us."

"I'm sure they will check our arrival time before leaving home, and the trains communicate by telegraph to the stations up ahead." Christopher pulled his heavy coat from the storage area.

"What are you doing?" Mother asked.

"I think we should get off the train for some exercise. The snow is slacking off, and we've been cooped up too long." Christopher held out Mother's coat for her.

"Do you think we could?" Mother asked. "I'd love to get on solid ground for a bit."

"I don't see why not."

"Will the train leave us?" Holly asked as she scrambled to find her coat.

"No, we'll have plenty of time to get back. They'll blow the whistle several times, and we'll tell the conductor that we're going." Christopher helped Holly find her hood and muff.

Mark didn't waste any time. This was a good chance to see a real western town. The sign over the station said Medicine Bow. An odd name, but maybe the residents of Medicine Bow would think the same about Minneapolis. One thing for sure, it was much smaller than Minneapolis. From the station platform Mark could see one wide main street with buildings on both sides. Even counting the side streets that he couldn't see, it was still small.

The air was cold, but the snow had quit completely. They walked briskly down the wooden sidewalk, looking in store windows as they went. There was a big mercantile and a smaller dress shop and an even smaller hat shop. Mark could see a bank and a livery stable as well. The street itself was quiet, with only a couple of buggies and a wagon pulled up in front of the mercantile. Horses stood, tied up, at hitching rails in front of the businesses. Other people from the train were out stretching their legs, too.

Mother and Holly stopped in the mercantile to browse, while Christopher went off to find a telegraph office to send a telegram to Uncle Abe saying that everyone was fine. Mark followed Mother and Holly for a while, but he soon tired of looking at the vast shelves of merchandise.

"I'm going to find Christopher," he called to Mother.

"Be careful," Mother said. "Don't get lost."

Mark rolled his eyes. How could a person get lost when there was only one street? He looked for the telegraph office, but before he found it, he was distracted by the appearance of three Indians. At least he was pretty sure they were Indians. They wore regular clothes except for the brightly colored blanket that one had thrown over his shoulders. Their hair was long, and their skin was a deep reddish-brown color. They must be Indians. Mark watched as they crossed the street ahead of him to go in the livery stable. Mark followed, hoping to get a closer look. Wouldn't Jens and Maureen be excited to hear that he had seen real Indians?

Just as he approached the livery stable, a girl about his age darted in front of him. She was chasing a small gray cat, which climbed a post right by Mark. He stopped to watch as the girl gently pried the cat's claws from the post and tucked him under her arm, scolding all the time.

"Hi. Who are you?" The girl looked at Mark with a friendly smile.

"Mark," he answered. "Did your cat escape?"

"Indeed she did. Lily is a bad cat." The girl shook her finger at the cat who just blinked. "I'm Melinda. Where you from?"

"Minneapolis," Mark said. "I'm going to San Francisco on the train. We're stuck until the snowplow engine comes through."

Melinda nodded. "Happens all the time in the winter, but this is supposed to be spring. Where you headed right now?"

Mark hesitated a moment before admitting that he was on the trail of three Indians. He wondered if Melinda would think he was a city dude.

"Must be Big Joe and his two boys. They're Shoshone Indians. I saw them earlier. Let me shut this cat up, and I'll take you to meet them." She ran to the side of a building where she opened a door and shoved the cat inside. "I live upstairs," Melinda explained. "My mother runs the hat shop."

"What does your father do?" Mark asked as they walked down the sidewalk.

"He was the sheriff, but now he's dead," Melinda said matter of factly.

"Sorry to hear that. Was he killed by outlaws?"

"No, he died of pneumonia. My mother said he always did have weak lungs for all that he was a good-sized man. She said that if he hadn't been so stubborn about bundling up in the winter, he'd still be alive." Melinda shook her head. "I don't think she really means it."

"My father died, too."

"I'm sorry. Some might say we've had bad luck, and others, that it was God's will. I'm never sure which is true. My mama says that God's in charge and has a plan even when we can't tell what in tarnation He's doing. I reckon she's right."

"Now I have a stepfather." Mark found this stranger easy to talk to.

Melinda pursed her lips and nodded. "I had a narrow escape with that once. The man who used to own the livery stable was courting Mama day and night. He wasn't a bad sort, but he smelled like horses all the time. I like horses, but I don't care to smell them all day long. Besides, I'm not so sure I want another father who could up and die on me. So I wasn't too sorry when Mama told him no. But, like I said, he wasn't a bad sort. Maybe I could have got used to the smell, and he probably would have given me my own horse."

"What happened to him?"

"He took his broken heart off to Laramie and married a schoolteacher six weeks later. What's your stepfather like?"

Mark shrugged his shoulders. "He's all right I guess. He tries to tell me what to do, but he does smell pretty good."

Melinda giggled. "Here we are." She turned into the door of the livery stable.

Off to one side sat a potbellied stove. The Indians and another man stood nearby with coffee cups in their hands. They looked up when they saw Melinda.

"What you up to, Melly?" asked the man who wasn't an Indian.

"Not much, Jem." Melinda motioned for Mark to follow her up by the stove.

"Who's your friend?" Jem asked.

"Mark. He's off the train. Waiting for the plow. I brought him to meet Old Joe and his boys. He's from Minneapolis. Hasn't met an Indian before."

Old Joe put down his coffee cup and stepped over to shake hands with Mark. His sons did the same. Their faces remained solemn but not unfriendly. Jem and Melinda talked for a few minutes and asked Mark some questions, but the Indians didn't say a word.

"Mark, we'd best be going," Melinda said eventually.

Mark followed his new friend back out onto the sidewalk. "Where are we going now?"

"I've got my doubts that you've seen a saloon, either," Melinda said. "I thought we'd mosey on over to the Silver Dollar Saloon."

Mark shook his head. "I guess not. I've walked by taverns in Minneapolis, but maybe that's not the same as a saloon. For sure I've never been in one."

"Likely we won't go in today," Melinda said. "My mama kind of frowns on that. We'll just peek in the window. That will be good enough."

"My mother would probably do more than frown," Mark said.

"Don't I just know it," Melinda said with a grin. "Mama says I sorely try her patience sometimes. Here we are."

The saloon was a big building toward the end of Main Street. It looked a lot like the other stores and shops except it had an extra big name sign over the front. Silver Dollar Saloon was in letters at least two feet tall. The hitching rail out front was bare. Mark guessed that any horses were warm in the livery stable.

"Let's see what we can see," Melinda said and pulled Mark up to the window. She shaded her eyes and put her face right up next to the glass.

"Won't someone see us snooping?"

"They don't pay no mind to nothing but their liquor and card playing."

Mark leaned up to look inside. The light was dim, but he could see two men leaning on the bar while a man in a white apron polished glasses behind it. A table of card players sat near the window, and several men stood around a piano where another man pounded out a tune.

Mark's eyes went back to the card players. "Well, I'll be," he said.

"What?" Melinda asked.

"I know one of those card players. I met him on the train, sort of met him, that is. He's a cardsharp. A real swindler according to my friend Rudy."

"You don't say. Now that's mighty interesting," Melinda said. "I wonder if Toby Ray knows that. That's Toby with the bushy brown hair. And that's Badger Thomas in the white shirt and Chester Bracken across from him." Melinda shook her head and frowned. "None of them's got a lick of sense or they wouldn't be gambling on a Monday afternoon. Still and all, I reckon that's no reason to let them get cheated."

"What can we do? Lucky Larry was friendly enough to me, but I doubt he'd appreciate it if we broke up his game."

"True. Let me think on this a minute."

Melinda's minute of thinking was interrupted with shouts from inside. They put their eyes to the window again and saw that the card players stood over Lucky Larry, yelling and shaking their fists. The man in the apron hurried from behind the bar.

"I think he's been found out," Melinda said.

The front door burst open, and Lucky Larry was escorted out by the aproned man. The door slammed, and the gambler tugged at his vest, straightened his jacket, and carefully placed his hat on his head. He saw Melinda and Mark when he turned. Without a word, he smiled, tipped his hat, and strolled off down the street.

"Well, I never," said Melinda.

"Mark! Mark Morgan!" Someone was yelling his name from across the street.

"I'm over here," he yelled back.

It was Rudy yelling, and Christopher was right beside him.

"Mark, where have you been? The snowplow got through sooner than expected," Christopher said. "Your mother said that you went to find me, but I had already left the telegraph office."

"I'm sorry," Mark said. "Melinda was introducing me to some Indians and then we saw Lucky Larry Peterson, and I didn't hear the whistle."

"Your mother is upset," Christopher said. "She's sure you've been kidnapped or worse. Why didn't you tell someone where you were going?"

"Gentlemen," said Rudy, "I suggest we sort this out after we get on the train. By my reckoning, that train will be pulling out in five minutes. Hopefully with us aboard."

"Let's go." Melinda took off. The others followed and reached the platform with time to spare. Mark stopped to wave at Melinda from the train steps before the conductor pulled him inside.

"Thanks for everything," Mark hollered through the window. It had been a grand afternoon, but now he had to face Mother. He didn't have to wait long, because she was standing right behind him with Holly. Her face was stern, but she didn't say a word, just motioned for him to follow her and Christopher back to the suite.

Mark made a face at Holly and fell in behind his mother. He might as well get his punishment underway.

CHAPTER 7
California at Last

"Mark, why on earth didn't you come back to the store when you didn't find Christopher?" Mother paced the carpet until Christopher took her arm. "We were so worried."

"I'm sorry," Mark said from his place at the table. "Things kept happening, and it didn't seem like much time had passed. I wasn't thinking, I guess." He looked straight at his mother. "I'm really sorry."

"I can accept that, but you'll have some time to help you think for the next day or so. You're confined to the suite for twenty-four hours. Meals and all. Schoolwork is your only occupation until this time tomorrow." Mother stopped her pacing and sank down onto a chair.

"Yes, ma'am," Mark said. He knew that if they had been

at home, his punishment would have been worse. It wasn't much of a stretch to see why his mother had been worried. He wasn't sure why he had forgotten about the train leaving. He wanted to blame Christopher, who had told them that the train wouldn't leave for hours yet, but that reasoning was way too shaky to try on his mother. Better leave well enough alone.

"If your mother agrees," Christopher said, looking at his wife, "maybe you could tell us about your adventures this afternoon."

"Did you see any Indians?" Holly yelled from the other room where she had been sent.

Mark glanced at his mother, who nodded. "Sure did. Three of them, but let me tell you about Melinda first."

He told them all about Melinda and Big Joe and his sons and even about Lucky Larry. He had to explain how he knew who Lucky Larry was, but Mother didn't seem upset. Holly wanted to stop on the return trip to meet Melinda, but Mother said she'd seen quite enough of Medicine Bow.

Mark had plenty of time to himself the next day or so, since the others didn't stay in the suite too much. He liked the quiet at first, but after awhile he was ready for company, even if it was just Holly.

But his sister had better things to do as the train steamed out of Wyoming and into Utah by late the next morning. Mark did some schoolwork and then stared out the window for five minutes before returning to his lessons. Ten minutes later he was looking out the window again. They had passed through the deep snow, and now the landscape was rocky and desolate.

Utah was much the same as Wyoming at first. In fact

Mark wouldn't have known they had crossed into Utah if Holly hadn't come to the suite to report what the conductor said.

"Why don't you ask Mother if you can come to the observation car later?" Holly asked. "Rudy says we'll be passing near the Great Salt Lake, and then later there will be desert to see. The observation car has big windows and chairs and couches. It's fun." Holly plopped down at the table across from Mark.

"I'd like to see it." He chewed his pencil for a moment. "Why don't you ask her?"

Holly grinned. "Coward!"

"I am not," Mark declared.

Holly just stared at her brother.

"All right, so I'm a coward where Mother is concerned." He wrinkled his nose at Holly. "Will you ask her?" This was one time when Holly's tendency to get her own way might work out for the best.

"I'll ask her, and if she says yes, you owe me plenty."

"Yeah, yeah. Just ask."

Holly persuaded Mother to let Mark come just to the observation car, so he was there in plenty of time to see the Great Salt Lake.

"It looks like a regular lake," Holly said, "but it's very big. You can't see the salt though, can you?"

"I hear tell that you can't sink in that lake," Rudy said. "The salt holds you up just like a glass of salty water will float an egg."

"It wouldn't be a good place for a murderer to dispose of a dead body then, would it?" Christopher said. "The body would pop right back up even if you weighted it down with bricks."

"Christopher," Mother said with raised eyebrows. "What a topic."

Christopher just grinned while the others laughed.

They spent the long afternoon talking and playing word games and watching the scenery flash by. A familiar strident voice sounded across the car late in the afternoon. Of course, it was the hat lady. Mark sank farther into his chair for fear that his body would somehow be propelled into the stout woman, but she passed by without incident.

Mark watched as the hat lady paused and looked around. Then she sat down by his mother and Christopher. Great. He tried to slide out of his chair. Time to retreat to the other end of the car.

"Mark." His mother's voice stopped his escape. "Come here and meet Mrs. Havington."

Mark obeyed and responded politely to the introduction. At least the hat lady had a name now. Mrs. Havington eyed Mark with a frown.

"You look familiar, boy. I've seen you somewhere before."

Mark didn't say anything that might remind her somehow of the dining car incident.

"Mark, look over here," Holly yelled as she darted among the chairs. "I think it's the—"

In her excitement she ran into her brother, and they both bumped Christopher, who reached out to steady the pair.

"Desert," she finished. Her eyes widened when she saw Mrs. Havington. "Sorry."

Mrs. Havington gave Holly a stern look when Mother introduced her to the woman. The hat lady nodded, said hello, and resumed her conversation with Mother.

Holly and Mark moved a few steps away.

"Come and look out this window," Holly said.

Mark did as she asked. The sun was going down, casting purple and pink and orange colors across the sky. He wished he had his camera with him so he could better remember the magnificent scene. Holly was right. It was the desert.

"A sight for sore eyes, that is," Rudy said as he came up behind them. "God's power spread out before us."

Mark could only stare at the display. He didn't have the right words to say what he felt.

The next day brought Nevada and many long miles of mountains and valleys and desert. Towns were few and far between. Mark and Holly spent most of the day exploring the train. It was their last full day on board, so they wanted to be sure to see everything.

Their train was scheduled to pull into Oakland around eleven o'clock on Thursday morning. From there it was just a ferry ride across the bay to San Francisco. Mark feared he'd have trouble sleeping Wednesday night because he was so excited. Holly babbled a mile a minute. But the now familiar rhythm of the train lulled him to sleep before Holly could wind down in her berth across the suite.

The train was already in California when Mark woke up Thursday morning. The Sierra Nevada stretched out like green waves with white snowcaps beyond the train windows. Mark had never seen mountains like the Sierra Nevada before. He dressed quickly, ate a hurried breakfast, and gathered up the last of his belongings. He and Holly went back to the observation car to watch California unfold. It grew much warmer as the sun rose higher. Spring had definitely come in California.

As they steamed through Sacramento and beyond, Holly

oohed and ahhed over the flowers that spilled out of pots on porches and peeked from gardens everywhere you looked. It was a different world than they had left in Minneapolis.

Before they could take it all in, the train was pulling into Oakland. Mother hustled Mark and Holly back to the suite so they could carry their smaller bags.

"I didn't get to tell Rudy good-bye," Holly said. "I can't leave without seeing Rudy."

"You won't have to, little lady." Rudy appeared in the door of the suite. "I'm taking the ferry across the bay, too. My sister is meeting me at the Palace Hotel. Bernetta and I are going to look around in the city for a week or so before we head for her home in San Jose."

"Oh, good." Holly grinned at Rudy. "You can meet our cousins."

The train slowed and stopped. Christopher led the way onto the platform. Before Mark had a chance to look around for his cousins, Mother was enveloped in a big hug bestowed by a well-dressed woman about her age.

"Judith!" Mother's voice was a girlish squeal as she held her cousin at arm's length and then hugged her again.

The next few minutes were a jumble of faces and voices. Mark met Cousin Albert and Judith, of course, and their children, Clifford, Curtis, and Caroline. All of the adults talked at once while the children smiled shyly at each other. Cousin Albert and Christopher went off at last to recover the rest of the luggage from the baggage car, and everyone else moved to one side of the platform to wait. Mother and Cousin Judith talked nonstop.

"I'll carry that for you," Clifford said as he reached for Holly's bag.

"Amanda Jean," yelled a familiar shrill voice from the other end of the station.

"It's Mrs. Havington," Holly hissed.

"Who's that?" Caroline asked.

"You don't want to know," Mark said.

"She's a grouchy lady from the train," Holly said.

Mother stopped talking to Judith long enough to glance over at the older woman, who was now standing with a young woman and two small children. "Mrs. Havington's daughter lives in Oakland, and I think her sister lives in San Francisco."

"Those poor grandchildren," Holly said.

"Tell us about her," Caroline said. "What happened on the train?"

Soon they were all chattering about the train trip.

In a few minutes Holly turned to Mark and asked, "Where is Rudy anyhow? I want Caroline to meet him."

"Right here I am, little lady," Rudy said as he walked up with Cousin Albert and Christopher.

Everyone had to meet Rudy, but eventually the group headed for the ferry dock. By noon they had boarded and were chugging across the blue water of San Francisco Bay. Mark and Clifford and Curtis went forward to hang over the railing and watch the city approach.

"Wow!" Mark said. "What is that building with the tower?"

"That's the Ferry Building," Clifford answered. "It's the tallest building in San Francisco. That's where we're headed. All the ferries go there."

Mark pulled his camera out of his pocket. "Here, you two stand so I can take your picture with the tower in the background."

"Take our picture, too," Holly yelled as she and Caroline raced to join the boys. Several pictures later, the ferry tooted its way up to a dock at the Ferry Building.

It took an hour to get all the baggage onshore and loaded into two carriages and a wagon. At last it was time to say good-bye to Rudy.

"We'll miss you," Holly said and gave the cowboy a hug.

"Thanks for everything," Mark said and shook hands with their new friend.

"Whoa, now, hold your horses, partners," Rudy said. "I don't aim to ride off to Texas without seeing you again."

"That's right," Christopher said. "We know where Rudy is staying. We've made some plans to get together."

"But for now we have to let Rudy be on his way to meet his sister," Mother said. "He's probably ready for a little peace and quiet."

Rudy just grinned, tipped his hat, and helped Holly into one of the carriages. "You be careful, little lady." He turned to Mark and leaned in to whisper, "No poker playing without me."

The cowboy stood on the curb and waved as they set out for the Dunlaps' home, which was several miles west of the waterfront.

"We're like a parade," Holly said as they made their way through the streets.

"A short parade," Mark stated. There were tall buildings on either side of the street. It looked a lot like downtown Minneapolis, with businesses and apartment buildings. After awhile there were houses instead of businesses. At first the houses were small and close together, but the farther west they went, the bigger the houses and lawns. One of the biggest differences from home was the steep hills that rolled in every direction. And then there were the cable cars that clanged their way up and down the hills.

"Do you ride on the cable cars?" Mark asked Curtis.

"All the time. We keep a carriage at the livery stable around the corner from our house, and we have an automobile ordered," Curtis said. "I was hoping it would arrive before you did, but no such luck. So for the meantime, we'll keep riding the cable cars everywhere."

"I can't wait to get a better look at them," Mark said. "We have streetcars but not cable cars in Minneapolis."

"We'll ride them when we show you around," Curtis said.

Caroline leaned forward to announce, "We got to miss school today to pick you up, and tomorrow we start Easter vacation. No school until at least next Tuesday. So that means we get to take you looking around tomorrow." Caroline turned to Holly. "I'm working on my mother to let us stay home until you leave. I think any good hostess would stay home with her guests." Her face crinkled in a crooked grin.

Holly giggled. "I think you're right."

"You two are birds of a feather," Mark said.

At that the two girls collapsed on the carriage seat in mutual giggles.

"We're home," Clifford said.

Mark looked up to see a big house that looked a little like his own and Maureen's. It was larger than Mark's house but smaller than Mrs. Figg's mansion. Like the Minneapolis houses, it had wide porches and a round tower room. The narrow lawn was short in front with a single tree and flower beds, but it looked much longer in the back. Mark saw the tips of several trees poking up from behind the house.

At the front door stood a dark-haired, smiling woman ready to meet them. "This is Margarite," Cousin Judith said. "She helps keep things running around here."

"Buenos dias," Margarite said, "I hope you like our city." She led the way inside the house.

The cousins spent the next couple hours getting settled in the big house and exploring. Holly was to stay with Caroline in her room, and Mark was sharing with Curtis, who at thirteen was closest in age to Mark. In no time they were all laughing and talking as if they had known each other for years rather than a few hours.

"I've got one last thing to show you," Curtis said late in the afternoon. "It's outside."

Curtis led Mark out the back door onto the lawn. A large brown dog bounded across the yard to meet them. "This is Captain." The boys petted the dog until he flopped down, panting, on the grass.

"This is what I wanted to show you," Curtis said and pointed up into a big tree.

Mark looked up. There, tucked among the leaves and branches, was a tree house. And what a tree house! With walls and a roof and a door, it looked like a tiny house that had grown up there in the air. A wooden ladder leaned against the broad trunk. Curtis adjusted it and climbed up.

Mark followed and found himself on a little porch with a railing. "I've never seen anything like this," Mark said. "Did you build it yourself?"

"My father and Clifford and I built it two years ago last summer." Curtis ducked through the small door.

Inside Mark saw a floor covered with a rag rug. There

were boxes for seating and other boxes for keeping things. Two windows had shutters that could be opened to let in light. Everywhere was evidence of projects and collections.

"You're lucky," Mark said. "My father was going to help me build a tree house. But then he died." Mark hadn't thought about that for a long time. He and his father had talked about the tree house several times that spring before Father died. That was probably the summer that Curtis and Clifford and Cousin Albert had built this tree house. Life wasn't fair.

"I'm sorry about your father," Curtis said.

"Yeah, thanks," Mark said and smiled.

"Maybe your new father will help you build a tree house," Curtis said.

"I don't really think of him as my father," Mark said flatly.

Curtis shoved a box over for Mark to sit on. "He still might help you build a tree house."

Mark sat down and looked out the window before answering. "Maybe, I guess." Or maybe not. Or maybe Mark didn't even want Christopher to help him. He wasn't sure.

CHAPTER 8

Cable Cars

It was a relief for Mark to go to sleep in a regular bed Thursday night and wake to the sound of birds singing and dogs barking rather than to the clacking of train wheels. He didn't waste any time getting dressed and downstairs to see what the Dunlap cousins had planned.

Breakfast was noisy, as everyone had a different idea about what to see first. "I vote for Fisherman's Wharf," Curtis said.

"What about Nob Hill?" Caroline asked. "I want Holly to see those fancy houses."

"Chinatown should be first," Clifford put in.

"Quiet!" Cousin Albert said. His children subsided. "Now,

if you three have finished, we'll get down to business. As the official tour guide on this excursion, I have some pronouncements to pronounce."

He gave them all an exaggerated fake frown when they laughed. "First, anyone here who is not my child is allowed to call me Albert. Although I suppose if my children really want to call me Albert, it can be negotiated."

"Father," Caroline said, "get to the point."

"Well said, my child, well said," Albert agreed. "Now where was I? Oh, yes, our itinerary. First we'll catch the cable car and ride it through Nob Hill. Then we'll stop at Old St. Mary's Church. Surely I don't need to remind you that this is Good Friday. We'll see if there is a scheduled service. If not, we'll have our own."

"That's a wonderful idea," Mother said. "We can't let the excitement of our trip overwhelm the sanctity of Easter."

"Exactly," Albert said. "The church is practically in Chinatown, so we'll take a look there and then reboard a cable car that will whisk us to Fisherman's Wharf."

"I hope you're including lunch in your itinerary, Albert dear," said Cousin Judith.

"I'm sure I'll be reminded of that at the proper time."

Mark felt a twinge of sadness as he listened to the Dunlaps trade jokes and opinions. It used to be like that at his house when Father was alive. In some ways Albert reminded him of Father. Perhaps it was because Albert was a banker like Father had been, or maybe because Albert was also deliberate and thoughtful.

Sad thoughts soon fled as the families trekked to the cable car stop. The sun had chased away some early wisps of fog, leaving a sunny spring morning. Mark didn't have to contain his curiosity about cable cars for long because one clanged its way up to the stop within a minute or two of their arrival.

"Thankfully, rush hour is over," Judith said, "or we might not all be able to get on the same car."

Mark crowded into a seat with Curtis and Clifford. "How often do the cars come?"

"Most of the time there's one every five minutes," Curtis said.

Mark leaned over to look at the man running the controls. "What does he do?" The uniformed man stood with his hands on a tall lever, which disappeared through a hole in the floor of the cable car.

"That's the gripman," Curtis said. "That lever is the grip."

"It catches hold of the cable under the street," Clifford added. "The cable pulls the car."

As Clifford talked, the gripman pushed the big lever forward. The car slowed and stopped.

"What makes it stop?" Mark leaned farther into the aisle to look at the slot he saw in the floor.

"When he pushes the lever forward, the grip releases the cable. All he has to do then is put the brakes on, and then we stop," Clifford explained.

Mark frowned as he listened. "But what about—"

"Look at that house!" Holly's voice interrupted Mark. "It's so big. And there's another one."

"This is Nob Hill," Caroline said.

"You said there were big fancy houses," Holly said, "but these are like palaces."

"That's true," Cousin Judith put in, "but the men who

own these houses are far from kings. For the most part they're ordinary men who made lots of money in mining or railroads." She raised her eyebrows. "Too much money for their own good, I'd say."

Mark looked from one side of the street to the other. The mansions were somewhat different in design but had one thing in common: they were all huge. Even Mrs. Figg's house wasn't this big. He wondered if any of these mansions with their dozens of rooms and towers and gables had a secret staircase like the one that he and Maureen had found in Mrs. Figg's house.

They all exclaimed their way through several blocks of the mansions before Albert called out, "Next stop is St. Mary's."

Mark still hadn't found out all he wanted to know about the cable car, so when the car slowed to a stop, he swung off and went quickly around to the front to lean down and look at the underside of the car. The lever did go right down into the street. The conductor was helping passengers off, so Mark walked up and peered into the slot in the street that ran between two rails. He couldn't see much, but he could hear movement.

Curtis joined him. "The cable is down there in a tube. It's an endless metal rope."

"What makes it go?"

"Steam engines turn big pulleys that pull the cable. I saw one of the powerhouses once," Curtis said. "They're at the beginning of each line—or the end, depending on how you look at it."

The cable car bell clanged loudly just a second or two before Christopher grabbed the two boys' shoulders.

"Cable cars have the right of way," he said, "even over curious boys."

Embarrassed at Christopher's having to grab him, Mark backed up to watch the car go on its way. Cable cars were almost as interesting as automobiles.

The church was right in front of them. Reddish brown in color, the church had a tall bell tower with a clock in it.

"Why do they call this Old St. Mary's?" Holly asked as they gazed at the building.

"There's a newer, bigger St. Mary's Cathedral over west toward Van Ness Avenue," Albert answered. "This one was built not long after the gold rush."

"Newer isn't always better," Cousin Judith said. "I've always loved this old church."

No Good Friday service was scheduled until noon, so the visitors looked at the inside of the church and sat down in a pew at the back. Albert and Christopher talked a little about Good Friday, and Mother offered a prayer. Mark liked the stillness of the church. He looked up at the big cross in the front. He didn't really like to think about how Jesus died. It sounded so awful. Much worse than how Father had died.

Albert's voice broke into Mark's thoughts. "The crucifixion was a part of God's plan for our salvation, terrible as it was. I used to wonder why God didn't choose a different way, an easier way, to save us. But now I know that God's plan is known only to Him. Sometimes we don't understand God's plan, but He wants us to trust Him anyway."

Mark looked at the pew in front of him. Understanding God was impossible as far as he was concerned.

In a few minutes they walked back outside.

"Now it's time for Chinatown," Albert announced. "We're right here at the gateway."

"Do we get to go in today, Father?" Caroline asked.

"Yes, I thought we'd walk a block or so while we look around and then catch the cable car again at Sacramento Street."

"Why wouldn't we go in?" Mark asked Curtis.

"Some people think it's dangerous."

"But it's not?"

"Father says it's no worse than any big city neighborhood and better by far than the Barbary Coast down by the waterfront," Clifford answered for his younger brother.

"Why do people think it's worse then?" Mark persisted.

"Lots of people hate the Chinese, so they always talk bad about them whether or not it's true," Clifford said.

While the boys talked, they had been walking north on Dupont Street. When Mark looked ahead again, words couldn't describe what he saw. The street was full of Chinese who were all in a hurry. Most of them wore black jackets and trousers and slippers with thick, white soles. Black felt hats sat on heads that sported long pigtails with vermilion braid intertwined.

Mark had the oddest feeling as he followed Albert and Clifford down the sidewalk. It was like a different country there, a different world even. The buildings were two and three stories tall, with balconies strung with giant lanterns. Most businesses displayed elaborately carved signs in front. Some of the roofs were peaked with upturned eaves.

"You look thunderstruck," Mother said at his elbow.

"I guess I am. This is so different," Mark said. "Why is it?"

"It's home to the Chinese. Home like the city of Canton

was to them before they came to the United States." Mother stopped to let a small pigtailed boy dart in front of her.

"So they tried to make it just like their old home," Mark said. "I think they must have succeeded." The words of their speech flowed over Mark like a warm river of sound offering no clue to their meaning, but friendly nonetheless.

They spent the next hour looking in some of the dozens of small shops. Mark saw carved jade and coral and ivory. All kinds of embroidered clothing and painted chinaware was for sale. Street peddlers and sidewalk merchants loudly announced their goods. He remembered that he had his camera and snapped pictures. He knew that he could never describe this scene to Maureen without pictures.

At last they made their way to the cable car stop with many small purchases stuffed in their pockets and bags. Mark bought a jade bracelet for Maureen and an ivory and coral brooch for Mrs. Figg.

Fisherman's Wharf wasn't far on the cable car, but by the time they arrived, everyone remembered that it was long past lunchtime. Albert led them to a small restaurant not far from the waterfront. Mark was starved.

Lunch didn't take long, and soon they were back outside walking along the wharf. Hundreds of boats were tied up there, and many more anchored in the bay to the north. The wharf itself bustled with activity as fishermen unloaded their morning's catch into carts and baskets.

The wind along the shore was brisk, and Cousin Judith had just announced that she was chilled to the bone and ready to leave for home when a noisy commotion erupted in front of them at a small shop. One of the raised voices reminded Mark of the hat lady's shrill tones, but a quick look revealed a woman who just sounded the same.

"I have no idea why you let these yellow dogs in your shop," the woman yelled at a man who was likely the store-keeper. "Any decent person would feel the same. That coolie was staring at me." She paused long enough to point a finger at a short Chinese man who stood quietly nearby, head bowed. A little girl clung to his hand.

"Ma'am, I'm so sorry," the storekeeper rushed to her side. "I'll take care of it." He turned to the Chinese man with a scowl. "Get out of here, now!" He put his hand on the man's shoulder and gave him a shove. The man stumbled, causing the little girl to trip and fall down. Quickly the man scooped the child up into his arms. She didn't cry, but Mark caught a glimpse of the terror in her eyes.

"Wait a minute," Christopher said. "What's going on here? You can't treat someone like that." He motioned for the Chinese man to wait.

"Sir," the woman said indignantly, "that coolie was accosting me."

"I beg your pardon, ma'am," Christopher said, "but he didn't accost you. He was trying to shop just like you are." Christopher glared at the storekeeper. "And he has just as much right to do that as anyone else."

He talked quietly to the Chinese man, who apparently understood some English. In a moment the man and Christopher bowed to each other before the man set the little girl on her feet and led her away down the street.

"Well, I never," the woman said. "Something really must be done about those yellow creatures and certain other people." She stuck her nose in the air and sailed off the opposite way.

The clanging of the cable car bell claimed Mark's attention. Everyone hurried the short distance to the stop and climbed on. They talked about the Chinese man and the little girl as the cable car carried them home. Mark didn't say much, but for the first time in a long while, he was able to look at Christopher and smile.

CHAPTER 9
Easter

"I've never seen fog so thick before," Mark said Saturday morning after breakfast. "You can't even see the house across the street." He was standing with Curtis at one of the front windows.

"We have lots of fog here," Curtis said. "Sometimes thicker than this. Probably it will clear out by noon."

"No need to go to the ocean today," Caroline said as she walked up behind the boys with Holly. "The beach would be damp and cold."

"We'll do something else," Curtis said.

"I know," Caroline piped up. "Let's go shopping. We could go downtown to the big stores. Wouldn't you like that, Holly?"

"Yes, I'd love to see the stores. Do you think we could?"

"Let's go ask right now," Caroline said. "My mother loves to shop."

"Now wait a minute," Curtis said. "I don't want to go shopping. Do you?" He asked Mark.

"Not really," Mark replied. Shopping was sometimes a necessity but never something a person did for entertainment.

"You two and Clifford can do something else," Caroline said airily as she sailed out of the room with Holly in her wake.

"Great," Curtis muttered. "Maybe our mothers won't give in."

"Holly generally gets her way," Mark said and shook his head. "The best we can hope for is that they'll leave us at home."

Curtis snapped his fingers. "I know what we'll do. Christopher can go with us somewhere else. I heard Father say that he had to go to the bank, but I know how to get places if Christopher will go with us."

"And I know what I want to see," Mark said. "You mentioned the place yesterday. It had an interesting name, but I can't quite think of it."

Just then Christopher strode down the front hall. Mark and Curtis ran out of the front room to ask him to go with them.

"So you've heard about the proposed shopping trip," Christopher said. "I'd love to go with you, but," he continued, "I've arranged some interviews this morning for my articles, since it's too foggy to go to the ocean."

"Oh," Mark said and turned away, unwilling to admit that he was disappointed.

"Perhaps Clifford could go with you two," Christopher

suggested. "At least to somewhere close."

"We could probably talk him into going somewhere," Curtis said. "Let's ask. Thanks for the idea, Christopher."

Mark followed Curtis, who ran toward the stairs. "I remember the name of the place I want to see," Mark said. "Let's go to the Barbary Coast."

"Hold it right there!" Christopher said and shut the front door that he had just opened. "Nobody is going to the Barbary Coast."

Mark and Curtis halted their flight and turned.

"Why not?" Mark asked. He frowned at Christopher's stern tone of voice. "You said we could go somewhere with Clifford."

"Somewhere that's not the Barbary Coast. That's the most dangerous part of San Francisco. It's full of dance halls and bars and gambling parlors along with the kind of people who frequent those places. It's no place for three young boys."

"We're not young boys," Mark said.

"I wasn't really thinking of going there," Curtis said.

Now Mark frowned at his cousin. Traitor. "We went to Chinatown," he persisted. "I thought the Barbary Coast was right next to it."

"It's nearby but a different section," Christopher said. "Besides, there were four adults in our group yesterday. A far cry from three boys. Mark, promise me that you won't go anywhere near that place."

"Oh, all right," Mark said. "I promise."

Christopher put his hat on and opened the front door again. "You can find something to do that's safer and closer. Have fun."

Mark plopped down on the stairs. *Have fun he says. How is that possible when you're treated like a child?* The admiration Mark had felt when his stepfather defended the Chinese man and child evaporated in the heat of resentment.

By afternoon the fog was gone as predicted. Clifford had disappeared to his friend George's house before Curtis and Mark could find him, so they were stuck at home while the women went shopping. They passed the time in the tree house, while Curtis tried to teach Mark how to play the harmonica. When they were all blown out, they looked at Clifford's stamp collection. It was a quiet morning, but fun.

"Why don't you like your new father?" Curtis asked as they sat eating sandwiches and apples for lunch.

"He's not my father," Mark said firmly. "But I like him all right, I guess."

"You don't act like it."

"He's always telling me what to do," Mark said. "I can figure stuff out for myself."

"My father tells me what to do all the time," Curtis said. "That's all that adults know how to do."

"Maybe, but like I said before, he's not my real father."

Curtis shrugged. It was clear to Mark that his cousin didn't understand, but it didn't matter. Mark understood about real fathers and stepfathers and knew the difference.

"Curtis, Mark," Clifford called from the foot of the tree. "Come on down, and we'll go look at the Octagon House."

The boys scrambled down the ladder. "What's the Octagon House?" Mark asked.

"It's an eight-sided house. The owners thought that the eight sides would bring luck," Curtis answered.

"Did it work? Bring luck, I mean," Mark asked.

"I don't know," Curtis said, "but it was built during the Civil War. Guess it's lucky to last so long. Say, Clifford, let's go to the park, too."

"Why not? But get a move on," Clifford said.

First the trio tramped north a few blocks to see the Octagon House, which was interesting but really just an odd-shaped house. Then they went back south to climb the hills of Lafayette Park. In Mark's opinion, it was an afternoon well spent.

Mark woke up early on Easter Sunday to the sun streaming in the window. No fog this day. After breakfast, the two families walked to services at the Dunlaps' church, which was only a few blocks away. As the sun warmed Mark's shoulders under his new suit, he found it hard to imagine that it was likely downright cold in Minnesota this morning. Here there were flowers everywhere and birds singing like it was June.

The church was much like Mark's church at home, which gave him a comfortable feeling. He had always loved Easter morning with its new clothes and joyous celebration of Christ's resurrection. Holly and Caroline looked like two plump little brightly colored birds as they sat down in the pew in front of Mark. They wore matching hats and dresses that they had wrangled from their mothers on Saturday's shopping trip.

The organ soared into the triumphant music that proclaimed the good news of Jesus risen from the tomb. The hair on the back of Mark's neck prickled as he listened to the choir sing. He felt closest to God when singing or listening to music, and today was no exception. Sometimes

Mark even suspected that the clue to understanding God and His ways might come through music, if it was possible to understand such things. For now, though, he was content to listen and enjoy and finally to worship.

After the service, they hurried home because a treat was planned in the visitors' honor. As soon as they could get changed and packed up, they were going by cable car to Golden Gate Park for a picnic lunch that Margarite had fixed before she went off to her church.

Everyone was in charge of carrying something. Even the girls were carrying a blanket apiece for spreading on the grass. Mark carried a jug of lemonade, while Curtis toted a couple of folding chairs for the mothers. Picnic baskets and boxes and sweaters loaded the others down.

"We should have taken a wagon," Cousin Judith said as they paraded down the sidewalk with all their equipment and food.

"Nonsense, dear. The cable car is part of the fun," Albert said as they swept up to the corner to wait for their ride.

"I'm not so sure about that," Cousin Judith said.

"There should be a surprise waiting for us at the park if plans go right," Christopher said.

"What kind of surprise?" Holly asked and gave her step-father a fetching smile that Mark knew was intended to pry out information.

"You'll not get the secret out of me," Christopher said with a chuckle. "You'll just have to wait."

Holly wrinkled her nose at him and flounced off to sit by Caroline after they climbed on the cable car.

"I wonder what he's talking about," Curtis said to Mark.

"Who knows," Mark said, "but if Holly can't get it out

of him, then nobody can."

The cable car was full of families with noisy children by the time they all hopped off in Golden Gate Park.

"How lovely," Mother said as she stared out across the acres of grass dotted with tulips and many other flowers. Shade trees were artfully placed throughout the park.

"All of this used to be sand dunes," Cousin Judith said.

"Unbelievable." Mother tore her attention away from the view. "Here, Holly. Give me that blanket."

In short order the mothers had claimed a shady spot under an oak tree, spread the blankets, and were getting the food out.

"I'll be back in a minute," Christopher said and walked toward a nearby building. The boys ran to look at a little pond at the bottom of a hill while the girls carefully arranged their things on the corner of one of the blankets.

"Don't run off," Cousin Judith called after the boys. "We're eating in a few minutes."

Mark reached the pond to see several toy boats floating across the water. Their tiny sails billowed in the breeze. Three young boys raced back and forth around the edge of the pond, chasing the boats.

"Looks like fun," Curtis said. "I wish Captain could have come with us. He loves to play in water."

"I bet he'd like to run across these lawns, too," Mark said.

"He'd probably jump right in the pond and chase the boats," Clifford said. "That would be something to see."

"Clifford! Curtis! Mark!" Mother's voice sang out down the grassy hill. "Come and eat."

Hunger drove the boys to abandon boating and run up the

hill. Lunch was laid out on the blankets and looked delicious.

"Where's Christopher?" Holly asked after they said grace.

"He should be back by now," Mother said.

A few minutes later Christopher appeared from around a bend in the nearby sidewalk. Beside him walked a familiar figure with a lady on his arm.

Holly squealed and ran to hug Rudy. The cowboy's big hat fell off as he leaned over to return Holly's hug.

"Howdy, ladies and gents," Rudy said. "It's right good to see you again." He leaned over to shake hands with Mark.

"You're a nice surprise," Holly said.

"Many thanks for your kind words," Rudy said. "Now let me introduce you to my sister, Bernetta."

Christopher handled the introductions, but by the time Bernetta met everyone, she was laughing and shaking her head in confusion.

Finally they settled down to eat and talk. Mark felt content as he lay on the blanket listening.

"I have a surprise of my own," Rudy announced as Mark and Curtis finished up lunch with big slices of cherry pie. They, along with everyone else, looked at Rudy expectantly.

"Well, I was cogitating on what I might come up with in the way of a treat for my new friends and their family. And I was thinking about how Mark is just right fond of music." Rudy paused to take a drink of lemonade. "And then, lo and behold, this opportunity just fell in my lap—or Bernetta's lap as the case may be."

"Rudy, get to the point," his sister said, nodding her head with each word.

"Yes, ma'am. The point being that Bernetta has been offered the use of a box at the Grand Opera on Tuesday night, and we want you all to join us." Rudy said the words as fast as Mark had ever heard him talk.

"The Grand Opera House!" Cousin Judith sat up straighter, and her eyes grew big. "That's the—"

"Metropolitan Opera of New York," Albert finished for his wife.

"But it's impossible to get seats," Cousin Judith said.

"Not when the theater manager is an old friend of Bernetta's," Rudy said. "Personally, I think he'd like to court her, but she says not."

"Rudy, you talk too much," Bernetta said sternly, but Mark could see her lips pressed together to keep from laughing.

"Some old fellow by the name of Caruso is top of the bill on Tuesday night," Rudy said. "Personally, I'd a sight rather see a good vaudeville show, but I'm willing to get a little culture."

"Enrico Caruso?" Mother asked. At Rudy's nod, she shook her head and chuckled. "Just the most famous singer ever."

"You mean we get to hear Enrico Caruso sing?" Mark asked. He had seen pictures of the famous Italian singer. In his wildest dreams, he would never have thought about actually seeing the man perform.

"I thought we'd all meet at the Palace Hotel, where Bernetta and I are staying, eat dinner, and then go to the Opera House to see this Caruso. What do you say, lad?" Rudy turned to Mark.

"I say yes," Mark answered immediately.

"So do I," Christopher said, "if everyone else agrees."

Everyone did agree, and soon plans were underway for

Tuesday night. After the food was picked up, the adults sat or lay on the blankets, lazily talking as the children drifted away to look around.

"What's that building over there?" Holly asked.

Mark looked where his sister was pointing and saw a large glass building with a dome and wings extending on either side.

"That's the Conservatory of Flowers," Caroline said. "Come on. I'll show you." She grabbed Holly's hand, and they skipped down a path toward the glass building.

"Is it a hothouse?" Mark asked as they followed the girls.

"A big one," Clifford answered. "It has all sorts of tropical flowers growing in there."

The boys had hardly reached the conservatory door before Holly was yelling for Mark.

"Come and look at this tree," she ordered, "and at these flowers."

"Looks like a palm tree," Mark said as he looked up at the tall, curved tree that had huge, long leaves bunched at the very top. "But I don't know what these purple flowers are."

"Orchids," said Cousin Judith, who appeared in the conservatory door followed by Mother and the others.

"They're beautiful," Mother said.

"Let's take pictures," Holly said. "Do you have our cameras in your bag, Mother?"

"That I do, and you've just given me an idea. We should take some group pictures. You take a picture of the palm tree and then we'll arrange ourselves over there by the orchids. Come on everyone."

Holly snapped her picture of the palm tree in just a moment, but it took much longer to arrange everyone for a group picture. With good-natured grumbling, they allowed themselves to be positioned and repositioned by Mother and Cousin Judith.

At last they were ready. First Bernetta took a couple pictures and then Mark took more so Rudy's sister could be in the photos as well.

Mark peered through the viewfinder as he moved to find just the right spot to stand. The smiling faces floated in front of him, but a sudden stab of pain went through him when he focused on Mother and Holly. Christopher knelt in the front row, balancing Holly on his knee. Mother stood behind with her hands on Christopher's shoulders. All three of them beamed at the camera.

It was wrong. Father should be in that spot, not Christopher. Mark stood there, stuck in the pain.

"Mark, take the picture," Mother demanded. "My face is cracking from this smile."

Mark clicked the shutter lever. The pictures were done, and soon they headed back to the cable car stop. Mark was glad, because the shine had gone off his day.

CHAPTER 10

The Great Caruso

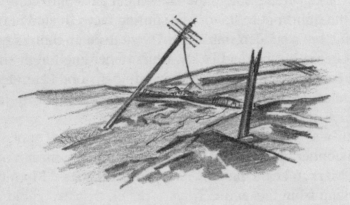

On Monday afternoon they went to see the Pacific Ocean. Mark's first glimpse of the great expanse that stretched before him brought a feeling of strangeness almost like a dream. The Great Salt Lake had been big, but always there had been a slight curving of the shoreline that suggested an end. The ocean looked as if it had no end at all.

Mark and Holly ran along the beach with Curtis and Caroline. Mark stopped to pick up shells and decided on the spot to start a collection. Holly filled a tiny bottle with sand to take home to Allyson and Carol. Seagulls dipped over the waves, and Mark thought he saw a sea lion on some rocks that jutted out from the beach. The cousins straggled home late in the afternoon, windblown and sandy, more than ready for an early supper and bedtime.

Tuesday should have been the day for the Dunlaps to go back to school after Easter vacation, but Caroline won the fight to take another day off. Christopher had more appointments and Albert went to work, but the others hopped on a series of cable cars to visit Mission Delores. Mark loved the simple chapel with its thick adobe walls and beautiful paintings on the walls. He knew that Maureen would also love this old building, so he took several pictures to show her.

Mother and Cousin Judith insisted on a short day of sightseeing so they could have plenty of time to get ready for the big evening at the opera. Mark didn't mind as he and Curtis spent a lazy afternoon in the tree house talking and looking at the shells they had found on Monday at the beach.

After much hustle and bustle, the families assembled in the parlor at six o'clock. Mark was disappointed that they were traveling in two carriages rather than by cable car. Cousin Judith had declared that people dining at the Palace Hotel did not arrive by cable car, no matter how convenient.

"I don't think I've been here before," Mark said when they reached Market Street, which was wide and angled off at a different direction from the other streets.

"I guess we haven't come this way yet," Clifford said.

"It's what everyone calls downtown or south of the slot," Curtis added.

"South of the slot?" Mark questioned.

"The slot between the cable car tracks on Market Street," Clifford said. "The cable cars don't really go into that part of town, so it's kind of a dividing line."

"It's not a fancy part of town, that's for sure, especially below Mission Street," Curtis said. "That's where the Opera House is, on Mission Street."

"Over there is the new City Hall," Curtis said and pointed at a tall domed building to the north.

"And then there's the U.S. Mint and the Post Office and the Call Building." Clifford reeled off the names as the carriage horses trotted briskly up the street.

"And now our fine tour is over because we are at the Palace," Curtis said.

The Palace Hotel was huge with brick walls and a grand facade. Inside, the restaurant glittered with crystal and candles and silver that sparkled against the crisp white tablecloths.

"There you are." Rudy's deep voice boomed across the lobby to Mark as he stood in the doorway of the restaurant with his family. A very different Rudy, if dress counted. The cowboy wore an evening suit and had shed his cowboy hat and boots. He hardly looked like the same old Rudy until his face cracked into the million-wrinkle grin.

"I have a table reserved," he said. "So let's get in there for some chow."

Holly and Caroline giggled, but each took one of Rudy's arms as he followed the uniformed and very correct waiter to their table near the center of the restaurant.

Soon they were eating California salmon as Mark tried hard to remember his best table manners. Faced with a wide array of forks and spoons and a knife or two, he watched Christopher, who sat beside him. His stepfather obviously knew which utensil to use for each type of food. For once Mark was grateful to be sitting next to him.

The waiter was placing a lemon ice in front of Mark for

dessert, when a hearty voice called, "Well, Mr. Wilkins. What a surprise."

Christopher turned. "A surprise indeed, Chief Dinan." He rose to shake hands with the man and a lady next to him.

"Let me introduce you to my family. This is my wife, Polly, and my son Mark and daughter Holly."

Mark didn't hear another word of the introductions. Christopher had called him his son. Not his stepson or his wife's son but his son. Mark stared into his bowl of lemon ice as if it would give him a clue as to what to think about this development.

"Mr. Dinan is the police chief in San Francisco." Christopher's voice broke into Mark's thoughts. "I interviewed him at City Hall yesterday about the automobile that he is using for police work. The chief is among the first to use an auto like that."

Chief Dinan beamed. "Thank you for your kind words, Mr. Wilkins. Now we'd best get to our table, or we'll be late for the opera. Wouldn't want to keep the famous Caruso waiting." He laughed heartily at his own joke and departed with Mrs. Dinan.

Mark turned his attention to his melting lemon ice. He wasn't going to think anymore about his stepfather on this exciting night. Seeing Enrico Caruso perform should be more than enough to keep his mind off his troubles.

The Grand Opera House was crowded with elaborately dressed women weighted down with jewels. The ladies were escorted by gentlemen in stiff white shirts and black coats. Rudy and Bernetta led the way to a box perched above the rows of seats on the main floor. As they sat down, the orchestra began the overture.

Mark's heart jumped as the music filled the barnlike Opera House. He sat on the first row in the box, so there was nothing to distract him as the curtain rose on *Carmen* and the great Caruso. Not that anything could have distracted him, so caught up was he in the performance. He blinked in surprise when the lights brightened at intermission. He couldn't believe that more than a few minutes had passed.

"Wasn't he wonderful?" Mother asked as they sipped punch from crystal glasses.

"He was," Albert agreed, "but I hear that Mr. Caruso can be quite the temperamental performer. Very demanding and emotional."

The lights dimmed, and soon the curtain went up again. Mark leaned forward in his seat a bit so as not to miss even a second of the performance. It wasn't just Caruso that he liked. The orchestra was equally spectacular. He thought of Jens and their school band and smiled. They had a ways to go.

Mark counted nine curtain calls for Caruso at the end of the show. He added his own enthusiastic applause to that of the others. By the time the families and Rudy and Bernetta had made their way out of the theater and said their good-byes, it was after midnight. Mark was glad he didn't have to go to school tomorrow. It was likely that Caroline would soon be begging for another day off for herself. Mark hoped she succeeded.

It was a quiet trip back to the Dunlaps' through silent city streets. High above, a bright star glittered in the sky over the carriage. Mark made a quick wish that tomorrow would be as wonderful as tonight had been. It was hard not to think about the fact that this trip was almost over, and Mark wasn't ready to go back to everyday life with its problems yet.

As the excitement of the evening subsided, Mark dozed off once, only to be startled when the horses shied suddenly. The carriage gave a jerk before Christopher, who was driving, could calm the excited animals.

The rest of the trip was uneventful, and soon they climbed out of the carriages in front of the Dunlap home. The horses were still nervous as they stamped their hooves and snorted.

"These animals sure are restless tonight," Albert said. "Come on, Christopher, let's take them back to the livery stable."

Mark wasted no time getting to bed. He wanted to think about the evening, but sleep overpowered him almost before he could get his pillow adjusted. The last thing he heard was a dog howling. It must be Captain, but Mark had never heard him bark at all, let alone howl in the middle of the night. It was a puzzle, but not enough to keep Mark from sleep.

It seemed only a few moments until Mark was shaken from his sleep. He found himself on the floor by the side of the bed that he shared with Curtis. At first he thought that he had fallen out of bed, which used to happen when he was small. Then he realized that the bed was moving and under him the floor bounced. What awful force had hold of him? He clung to the floor as best he could, but it bounced harder yet.

He heard a low rumbling sound, and seconds later the room began to sway. The floor went side to side at the same time that it bounced. Everything in the room was in motion, flying off all surfaces to land in a jumble on the floor. The sound of breaking glass came from all directions. Then the swaying eased a bit, but the bouncing continued.

Curtis crawled around the side of the bed. "Quick, we've

got to get in the doorway." He grabbed Mark's shoulder.

"What is it?" Mark hesitated only a moment in confusion before crawling with his cousin over to sprawl in the open doorway.

"An earthquake!" Curtis said.

Curtis had barely finished speaking before the horrible sideways shaking began again. If possible it was even more violent. It was early morning because the light barely came in the east window.

More crashes echoed through the room as something big hit the floor. As the shaking subsided, Mark saw that huge chunks of plaster from the ceiling had fallen. The dim light grew even dimmer as the room filled with a haze that looked at first like smoke. But the taste in Mark's mouth wasn't smoke. It was dust, plaster dust. Terror rose in his throat. "Will the house fall over?" he croaked through dust-coated lips.

"I don't think so," Curtis said. "It never has, and we have earthquakes all the time."

"Like this?" Mark said in amazement.

"No, definitely not like this."

"Boys!" Albert appeared in the dusty hallway over them. "Get your pants and shoes and get downstairs, fast."

The boys scrambled to obey and in a minute or less sat with the rest of the household members on the front sidewalk. Holly and Caroline clutched one another and their mothers as they all huddled together.

"Please, let's pray," Mother said in a shaky voice. They all knelt or stood in a small circle and joined hands. "Please, our Father," her voice grew stronger, "please protect us from this upheaval. We put ourselves in Your hands. Give us strength to endure whatever comes. We pray this in Your Son's name. Amen."

As Mother finished, another tremor began. Mark braced himself, but this time the shaking was gentle. Mark heard a new sound. Bells were ringing. The ringing drifted over the city and slowly faded as the tremor did. He looked up at Christopher, who still stood over him.

"It's church bells," Christopher said. "The quake is ringing them."

Mark shivered, and it wasn't from the early morning chill. Was God sending a message to His people? Mark thought about those bells more than once during the next couple hours.

As time passed, it looked like the worst of the tremors were over. Now and again the ground would vibrate or even shake, but the intensity lessened each time. Finally Albert and Christopher went into the house to fetch blankets and clothes for everyone who hadn't had time to grab anything. Everyone else stayed out in the open.

All around the neighborhood were similar scenes, and within minutes people started walking up and down the street. Mark felt dazed, but when his stomach growled, he found that he was also hungry. Then he wondered about the rest of San Francisco. Had it been damaged, too?

Caroline solved the hunger issue. She stood up and announced, "Earthquake or no earthquake, I'm hungry."

Everyone laughed, glad to be distracted by everyday problems. Cousin Judith hugged her daughter and declared that she was right sharpish herself.

"It's time to raid the pantry," she said. "You stay right here, and I'll see what I can find." With that she stomped around the house toward the back door, with Albert close behind.

In a few minutes they feasted on bread and jam washed down with a jug of milk poured into mugs Cousin Judith had toted from the kitchen in the picnic basket.

"There's plenty to eat in there," Cousin Judith said. "We'll just have to find a way to cook it outside, because I'm not going in the house long enough to cook until we're sure this shake is over."

Christopher walked around from the side of the house. "I don't see any obvious structural damage to your house," he said. "I'm no expert, but the foundation looks solid— without any cracks. Of course the chimney's down and the inside is a mess, but I'd say that you're in pretty good shape, all things considered."

"I hope everyone else is as fortunate," Mother said.

"Perhaps I should walk a few blocks toward town and see if the damage is the same there," Albert said.

"May we go, too?" Curtis was quick to ask.

"I don't know about that," Cousin Judith said. "I doubt that Polly wants Mark wandering the streets."

"Not by himself, but I suppose he could go with Albert," Mother said. "I know someone else who is probably anxious to get a look at everything." She smiled up at Christopher, who leaned over and gave her a quick kiss.

"I wouldn't want to leave you alone," he said.

"We'll be fine. Go on and see if you can find out any news." Mother patted his cheek.

"Let's go over to Lafayette Park," Clifford said. "It's so high that we ought to be able to see what's going on in the rest of the city."

"Excellent idea, Son," said Albert.

Mark was pleased to join the men, but his pleasure faded as they walked the few blocks to Lafayette Park. It was soon clear that the Dunlaps had been fortunate indeed. Many homes had much more damage. Their roofs were partly fallen in and their walls had crashed. Mark saw people sitting on the curb in their nightclothes and others wandering with a bewildered look on their faces. It was frightening, yet he wanted to see more.

The big mansions that ringed the square looked fairly intact. That was reassuring, but the sight that met his eyes when they climbed to the highest point in the park and looked east and south was not.

Mark gasped when he looked out over the sea of buildings that stretched to the bay that they had crossed by ferry just a few days ago. Here and there huge plumes of smoke billowed into the blue sky. To the southeast, toward the Palace Hotel and the Grand Opera House, Mark saw a solid wall of smoke. Its base flickered with red and orange flames. San Francisco was on fire!

CHAPTER 11

A Long Day

"Did the earthquake cause the fire?" Mark found his voice to ask. He couldn't tear his eyes away from those plumes of smoke that billowed straight up into the windless blue sky.

"I'm not sure," said Albert. "It must have because there are several different fires. They wouldn't have all started from regular causes."

"Maybe it was broken gas mains," Christopher said.

"But the fire department will put them out, won't it?" Mark asked.

His stepfather hesitated a split second before answering.

"Of course it will," he said and put his hand on Mark's shoulder. "San Francisco has a topnotch fire department."

"The best," Albert said. "If anyone can stop those fires, our firemen can."

"I hope they're doing it right now," said Curtis.

"So do I, Son," Albert said. "So do I. We'd better get back home before the women worry."

Mark hurried with the others back to the Dunlap home. The fires gave him a bad feeling, but it was hard to turn away from watching them.

Mother and Cousin Judith were hard at work with Caroline and Holly as willing helpers. They had dragged a big table out into the backyard and were piling it with cooking supplies and utensils. Holly was raking a smooth spot in a flower bed in the middle of the lawn, and Caroline was stacking some wood nearby. It looked like they were building a fire.

Christopher walked up to Mother and pulled her close. "You ladies have been busy."

Mother smiled up at him. "I'm glad you're back. What did you see?" The others all gathered by the table.

"We saw fires," Mark burst out. "Several."

"Oh, no," Mother said softly.

"Christopher says the fire department will put them out," Mark said.

"Not if they don't have any more water than we do," Cousin Judith said. "The water from the faucets is down to a trickle now."

"I was afraid of that," Albert said soberly. "The water mains must be broken."

"What will we do?" Curtis asked.

"We'll be fine," Albert said. "We've got that old cistern up by the house. We'll just dip out of it." He looked back to the southwest. "But that won't help them down there."

Mark followed Albert's gaze. Now the smoke was visible high in the sky. The day was growing warm, but Mark felt a chill go over him. What if there was no water for the firemen? How far would a fire like that burn before burning itself out?

There was work to do, so everyone pitched in. Albert and Christopher fixed an old iron grill over the fire that Clifford had built in the dirt of the flower bed. Mark and Curtis hauled water from the cistern while Mother and Judith finished rounding up some pots and other supplies. Holly and Caroline spread a blanket under the big tree with the tree house and stacked some other blankets and towels on it.

Mother and Cousin Judith fixed an early lunch of fried ham and potatoes that tasted like steak to Mark. He felt much better after eating.

"Albert, I'm worried about Margarite," Cousin Judith said while they were still sitting around the table. "You know she would have been here this morning if she could have. Her daughter's house is on Tenth Street, the other side of Market. Could the fires go that way?"

"I doubt it," Albert said, "but why don't Christopher and I take a hike down there. We'll check on Margarite and find out what's going on with the fires."

"We'll get things finished up here," Cousin Judith said. "Do you think we'd better sleep outside tonight?"

"Maybe, just to be safe," Albert said. "The tremors are coming less often now, but it won't hurt to spend tonight outside." He smiled at his wife. "You and the children can set up camp."

Mark frowned as he walked around the table to stand by his mother and Christopher. "Are you sure you should go there? It's dangerous."

"I was thinking the same thing," Mother said, "but I'm sure they'll be careful."

"We will be. I promise," Christopher said. "We've got to find out what's happening so we'll know what to do next." He bent over to hug Holly, who had leaned up against him. "Don't worry, but it's fine if you want to pray every once in awhile."

In a few minutes the two men hiked east to Van Ness Avenue, where they would head south. Mark watched them go. He wanted to know what was happening, but he didn't like Christopher and Albert being separated from the rest of the family. In the back of his mind was a nagging fear. What if something should happen to Christopher?

Within the next half hour, word of the earthquake damage and fires spread through the neighborhood. People congregated in the street and talked. Mark and Curtis went from group to group, listening to the tales of destruction. One man had been on his way home from work when the quake hit. He told of entire buildings collapsing, of people trapped in the debris, and of a little girl snatched from her dead mother's arms.

Mark couldn't listen anymore. He sat on the curb and stared off to the southeast, where the smoke still billowed into the sky from unseen fires. Curtis sat down beside him. They didn't talk. In a moment another stronger tremor shook the earth. Mark grabbed Curtis's arm. They didn't move but sat, waiting, until that tremor eased like the others.

"There you two are," said Cousin Judith from the sidewalk near the front porch. "Curtis, would you please run next door and see if Mrs. Temple needs anything? I asked her earlier to come and join us, but she insisted on staying at home. I urged her to stay outdoors for a few hours at least, but she said that there was work to be done." Cousin Judith frowned. "I'm not sure she was thinking clearly, but she's a strong-willed woman. If you boys stop in, she won't think that I'm trying to check up on her."

"Do we go inside?" Curtis asked.

His mother hesitated. "Just for a minute, and if you feel a tremor, get back outside."

Curtis and Mark ran across the lawns to Mrs. Temple's porch. The front door stood open, but the hallway was empty. Curtis called her name, and someone answered from the back of the house. The boys picked their way down the plaster-strewn hallway and found Mrs. Temple seated at the dining room table. All around her on the floor were broken dishes, evidently thrown out of several glass-fronted cupboards toppled in the quake.

"How nice to see you, Curtis, and this must be your cousin."

"Yes, ma'am. Do you need anything?"

"Please sit down, boys." Mrs. Temple waved at the chairs that were still tipped or fallen. "I'm just doing a bit of mending."

In front of Mrs. Temple sat a glue pot and one china plate. Mark looked more closely. She had a pile of china fragments on one side and the piece of plate on the other. She was gluing the pieces together, or at least she was trying to glue them. It looked like an impossible task. Mark looked at Curtis, and they both looked at the thousands of pieces of china scattered everywhere.

"Let me get you young men a cup of tea," Mrs. Temple said and jumped up. "This mending has given me a thirst."

"Oh, no, that's not necessary, Mrs. Temple," Curtis said. "Don't go to any trouble."

"Oh, lands sake, it's no trouble," the woman said as she disappeared down the hall. "I'll just get the fire going and heat water for tea."

"Do you think she's acting normal?" Mark asked.

"I don't know," Curtis replied. "She's always been a little odd, but this seems different. As if anyone could mend all of this broken china." Curtis shook his head. "I better tell Mother."

There was a clatter and a thud from the direction of the kitchen. "I wonder what she's doing?" Mark asked with a frown.

"Fixing tea, I guess."

"Starting a fire," Mark said slowly and stood up. "She's starting a fire!" His voice grew louder with each word.

"The chimney," Curtis yelled. "There's no chimney!"

They turned and ran down the hall to the kitchen, crunching through the china fragments as they went.

Mrs. Temple was just closing the door of the cookstove. "We'll have tea in a minute, boys."

Mark yanked open the stove door. There was a small fire crackling merrily. "Quick, close the damper," Mark shouted to Curtis, who reached up and flipped a lever on the stove-pipe. Mark grabbed the tea kettle from the top of the stove, pulled the lid off, and tossed the water at the fire. With a sizzle, the fire sputtered out.

"Oh, my," Mrs. Temple said. "If you didn't want tea, you should have said so."

"No, ma'am, it's not that," Curtis said and pulled a stool up by the stovepipe. "Your chimney is down like all the rest in the neighborhood. Starting a fire in the stove could catch your whole house on fire if the chimney was blocked up above."

"Oh, dear," Mrs. Temple said, "I didn't think of that."

Curtis climbed on the stool and reached up to feel the stovepipe where it went into the chimney.

"Is it hot?" Mark asked.

"No, it's barely warm," Curtis said. "I think we caught it in time."

Mark let out a big sigh of relief. This was too close a call for him.

"Mrs. Temple," Curtis said, "you come back to my house. My mother will fix you a cup of tea outside on the campfire."

"But I should be mending that china," she said.

"It will wait, ma'am," Mark said and held out his arm for her to take. "Let's go get that cup of tea."

Back at the Dunlap house, Mother fixed a cup of tea for Mrs. Temple while Curtis and Mark took Cousin Judith aside and told her what had happened. She took a deep breath and shook her head.

"Thank you, boys," she said in a low voice. "I'll take care of her now."

Mark and Curtis sank down on the blanket under the big tree. Holly and Caroline appeared to hear what had happened next door. As they talked, a horn beeped from the front of the house. Mother remained at the table talking to Mrs. Temple, but everyone else went around the side of the house.

Out in the street, Mark saw a big automobile, engine purring. The driver was a young man, and the passengers were a man and a woman.

110

"It's our friends, the Jacksons, from down the street," Curtis said, "and their son. I think he lives south of the city somewhere."

"William, Millicent," Cousin Judith said, "Albert told me that you were fine when he checked earlier, but it's good to see it with my own eyes."

"Harry has come to take us to his house," Mrs. Jackson said. "The damage there is less, and there are no fires. We wondered if you want to send the children with us, and then Harry will come back for everyone else. Who knows what will happen here."

"That's kind of you, Millicent, but we'll be fine. Albert and Christopher will be back any time now. But you know, I wonder if you could take Mrs. Temple." Cousin Judith moved closer and related the fire incident.

"Oh, my. Harry turn this vehicle around and park in front of Mrs. Temple's house while I go talk to her." Mrs. Jackson climbed out of the auto and walked with Cousin Judith around the house.

The boys watched as Harry did as his mother commanded.

"That's some auto," Mark said. "I'm not sure I've ever seen one like it before."

"You should see Mr. Jackson's auto," Curtis said. "It's brand new. I wonder why he's not driving it."

The two men stepped out of the auto and walked over to stand in the shade of a tree.

"Where's your auto, Mr. Jackson?"

Mr. Jackson made a face. "There's a fallen tree blocking the shed door. I can't budge it. I wanted to get the ax at it, but Millie wouldn't hear of that."

"You can get it later," Curtis said.

"If there is a later," Mr. Jackson muttered as he looked to the southeast.

Mark looked, too. The smoke appeared thicker and certainly wider. Thoughts of autos fled as he watched. Surely Christopher and Albert would be back soon with news.

Mrs. Temple was persuaded at length to pack a small bag and go with the Jacksons. Cousin Judith and Mother returned to the backyard, where they had put a pot of stew on the campfire to simmer.

Mark and Curtis returned to their spot on the curb to watch for Albert and Christopher. Mark noticed that Mother came to the side of the house once in awhile to look east. Her face was tense, but when she saw Mark looking at her, she smiled and went back to stirring the stew.

More and more people came down the street. Many of them did not appear to be from the neighborhood. Some carried bags or pulled wagons of belongings. A few were Chinese, and all trudged wearily west.

An old lady dropped her bag right in front of the boys. After they helped her pick up her things, Curtis asked her where she was headed.

"To the Presidio. It's the only safe place. I've got to get there." She thanked the boys and resumed her trek.

"The Presidio is an army garrison west of here," Curtis said before Mark could ask. "I wonder why she thinks she needs to go there?"

"That must be where they're all going," Mark said.

Clifford walked up as they were discussing this latest turn of events.

"Where have you been?" Curtis asked. "You've been gone for hours."

Clifford's clothes were covered with dust, and his face was pale. "I was at my friend George's house." He rubbed his forehead. "George's father was trapped when a wall fell on him just a little while ago. I helped dig him out. He was hurt."

"Will he be all right?" Mark asked.

"I don't know. It looked bad to me." Clifford flopped down on the curb. "They took him to the hospital at the Presidio."

Mark stood up. "Let's walk a ways and look for Christopher and your father." Suddenly it seemed critical that he know that his stepfather and cousin were safe. Surely they would return soon with some news.

CHAPTER 12

On Fire

Curtis saw them first. He grabbed Mark's arm, and they ran down the street to meet Christopher and Albert, who plodded wearily toward the boys. The men's faces were grimy, and their clothes streaked with dirt and sweat.

"What happened?" Mark asked.

Christopher's face sobered as he slowly shook his head. "The devastation is unbelievable."

"Unbelievable," Albert echoed.

"There you two are," Mother said from the side of the house. Her eyes swept over Christopher and finally she smiled. "Come have some cold water and tell us what you saw."

Everyone gathered around as the men sat down at the table in the backyard.

"What's it like?" Cousin Judith asked as she poured water into mugs for them.

Albert looked up at the sky briefly. "I'm not sure if I can describe what we saw."

114

"A huge section of the city is burning," Christopher said, "and there's almost no water to fight the fires."

"The firemen go from hydrant to hydrant," Albert said, "but they're all dry. Occasionally they'll find a cistern or tank to pump from, but it barely slows the spread."

"What about Margarite?" Caroline asked.

"We couldn't get into that section, but her daughter's house is certainly burned," Albert said and pulled Caroline close. "From what I could find out, that section didn't catch fire immediately after the quake. Which probably means that Margarite and her daughter and family had time to get out."

"They're evacuating people from the Ferry Building," Christopher said. "So thousands of people are fleeing to the foot of Market Street at the waterfront. The ferries take them across the bay to Oakland. I imagine that's where Margarite is."

"I hope so," Caroline said with a frown.

"How did you get so dirty?" Holly asked.

"We were trying to find out about Margarite and got between two arms of the fire. One arm is burning east and another southwest," Christopher said. "We turned around when we realized what was happening, but we came upon some firemen trying to rescue a man and woman trapped in their collapsed house. The fire was roaring toward them, so we stopped to help."

"Did you rescue them in time?" Mark asked.

"Yes, we did," Albert said, "and we've only the good Lord to thank for that. I felt like my tail feathers were getting singed by the time we got that couple to safety."

"Will the fires meet and burn themselves out?" Mother asked.

"They might if those two lines were the only ones, but

they're not," Christopher said. "One of the firemen told us that there is a separate fire traveling north through the financial district. He said it's possible that it might turn west. Depends on the wind and if they can find water or some other way to stop it."

"Toward Nob Hill," Clifford said.

"That's possible," Albert agreed.

"But that's our direction," Curtis said.

"It would be traveling in our general direction," Albert conceded, "but Nob Hill is a long way east of here. We'll confine ourselves to more immediate worries. Is that stew I smell? I'm famished."

Soon they all gathered around the stew pot with bowls and spoons. Except for Mark. He didn't feel hungry and went to the curb in front once more. Darkness was coming, and when he looked to the east and southeast, he could still see the smoke, but now an orange glow was barely visible. He could also smell smoke, which he hadn't noticed before. It was hard to believe that just last evening he had been at the opera watching Caruso. Where was Caruso? For that matter, where were Rudy and his sister? So much trouble in so short a time.

The flow of people traveling in front of the house had increased from a trickle to a steady stream. Mark listened for a moment. He heard Chinese spoken and another language he couldn't identify. The people didn't talk much. They put most of their energy into limping and straggling and dragging themselves west. Burdened down with belongings, they sometimes stumbled or stopped to adjust their loads.

An old Chinese gentleman fell to his knees in front of Mark, who ran to help him. The man was traveling alone and seemed exhausted if not ill. Mark lifted him gently by the arm and helped him over to the curb to sit. When the old man didn't respond to Mark's questions, Mark gestured for him to remain where he was. Then Mark went to the corner of the house and yelled for his mother and Christopher.

Soon the old man was sipping a cup of water while resting on a blanket that Cousin Judith spread on the front lawn.

"I didn't realize so many people were going past here or that they were in such bad shape," Cousin Judith said. "Look at the cut on this man's head. He needs medical attention, but I doubt he'll make it to the Presidio."

"I'll get some ointment and bandages," Mother said. "Mark, you and Holly get some more water and bring it around here. At least we can offer these people a drink when they go by."

The next couple hours were so busy that Mark and Holly forgot to watch the fire most of the time. Everyone had work to do. The front lawn gradually filled up with refugees who couldn't go another step. Some had been injured in the earthquake, and others were very old or very young. All were grateful to sink down on the blankets that the families spread on the grass.

Mother and Cousin Judith moved from one refugee to the next, treating injuries as best they could. Albert and Christopher went through the house, collecting more blankets and towels and other supplies. The boys carried water, while Holly and Caroline dipped the liquid into hands and cups of the fleeing crowd.

"Why are there so many Chinese going past?" Mark asked.

"A woman told me that Chinatown is right in the path of the fire burning north," Cousin Judith said. "The soldiers told the Chinese to get out while they could."

Mark remembered the lively, colorful world of Chinatown that he had seen last week. Now it might be in flames, gone forever.

By eight o'clock, Mark was longing for a bed but glad to settle for a blanket on the lawn. Last night had been very short, and his whole body ached from fatigue. At last Mother and Cousin Judith sent all the cousins around back to stretch out on the blankets by the campfire. A chilly night meant more blankets were needed, so Albert and Christopher went over to Mrs. Temple's house to see what they could find.

Mark and Curtis made one last trip from the cistern with water for the passing crowds. They put the buckets on the curb with dippers so anyone could stop for a cool drink as they walked past. The flow of people was as steady as ever. They talked less, but the rattle of carts and wagons and the shuffle of feet were constant. Once in awhile a horse and wagon or carriage would clatter by and very occasionally an automobile passed, but mostly it was just people, hundreds and hundreds of them.

Mark carefully balanced the dipper handle on the edge of the bucket and raised up to stretch his aching back.

"Howdy, partner," a voice said out of the darkness in the street. "Got any water for some weary travelers?"

Mark jerked around to see Rudy and Bernetta walking toward him out of the crowd. "Rudy!" He ran to the couple. "I'm so glad to see you. Are you all right?" The cowboy had lost his big hat and was dirty and bedraggled from head to toe. His sister didn't look much better, but both were smiling.

"We're fine now that we see that you are, too," Rudy said.

"All of the family is in one piece, but I can't say that for some of these people." Mark waved in the direction of the lawn with its flock of blankets laden with refugees. "Mother! Look who's here."

In moments Rudy and Bernetta were surrounded by the whole family. Mark felt his heart lighten with this one bit of good news. After a bowl of stew, the couple settled on a blanket to tell what had happened to them since the quake.

"The old Palace Hotel is gone, burned," Rudy related. "They kept it from burning for a long time by using its own water tanks, but that couldn't last forever. I heard that it burst into flames at the end. By then we were knee deep in trouble over at the Mechanic's Pavilion."

"The rescue workers had taken most of the badly injured to the pavilion right after the quake, because at least two hospitals were destroyed," Bernetta said. "We went there to help."

"Bernetta here has some nurse's training," Rudy said, "and I have a strong stomach, so we thought we could help. Everything was going about as well as you could expect, given the circumstances, when some fool woman over on Hayes Street set her chimney on fire trying to light a stove."

"Before you knew it, that fire was bearing down on the Mechanic's Pavilion," Bernetta said. "All the injured had to be evacuated."

"They put them in wagons and some in automobiles that the military had taken over from people," said Rudy. "After they were all on their way to Letterman Hospital at the Presidio or to the camp in Golden Gate Park, we decided to light out of there. And here we are."

"And glad we are to see you," said Cousin Judith. "We'll find some clean clothes for you, and then you can get some sleep. We're staying outside tonight, but if there aren't any major aftershocks in the night, I'm determined to move back into the house in the morning."

"I would welcome a change of clothes," Bernetta said, "but then I'll help you with your visitors. Perhaps we can nap a bit later."

"We won't argue with you," Mother said. "We could use

119

an experienced nurse's opinion about some of these injuries. But you children go around back and bed down. I'm afraid we're going to need even more help by morning."

"They just keep coming, don't they?" Christopher said. A clatter in the street and agitated voices told the tale of yet another refugee collapsed and in need of help. Christopher and Albert picked up a nearby lantern and investigated.

Mark dragged himself around back and dropped onto a blanket. He barely had time to pull another on top before he fell asleep.

He woke with a start early Thursday morning when a small tremor shook the ground under his blanket. It was quickly over, but he was wide awake. Rolling over, he saw that the sky overhead was brightening with dawn. Might as well get up.

He could tell without looking that the fires were still burning. The air seemed hazy and had an odd color as it grew lighter. When Mark walked around the corner of the house, he looked east and gasped. Practically the whole eastern horizon glowed orange. He saw Mother leaning over an old woman who lay on a blanket near the front curb. "Mother!"

Mother looked up and smiled at him. She looked tired and pale. "Good morning, dear. Did you sleep well?"

"The fires," he said, ignoring her question. "They're so much bigger and closer."

Mother straightened up and put her hands on her back as she walked over to Mark. "Don't worry. The soldiers from Fort Mason and the Presidio are helping fight the fires. I'm sure they'll get them under control soon."

A muffled boom came from the east. Mark looked but couldn't see anything but fire. "What was that?"

"It may be dynamite. Christopher and Albert went with

Rudy over to Van Ness Avenue to see if there was any news. Christopher thinks they're using dynamite to try to stop the fires. The booms have been sounding for a while now." Mother pushed her hair out of her face. "I just pray that something will work."

In a few minutes the men returned. By then the others had awakened and gathered around.

"It is dynamite," Christopher said. "They're blowing up houses in advance of the fires to create a firebreak."

"Will it work?" Clifford asked.

"It might, if they knew what they were doing," Albert said.

"They're mighty short of explosives experts from what we heard," Rudy said. "I guess Fire Chief Sullivan was the department expert, and he's lying in Letterman Hospital in a coma. The fire house fell in during the quake and took him with it."

"Poor man," Mother said quietly, "may God care for him and his family."

"Where are they blowing up houses?" Curtis asked.

"On the east side of Van Ness. It's the widest street in the city, and the firemen hope to hold the flames there. Blow up the houses, and it takes away the fuel," Albert said.

"Or would do that, if the dynamiters knew what they were doing," added Christopher.

"Sometimes they wait too long to use the dynamite," Albert said. "Then the fire is too close, and it doesn't do any good."

"And when they run out of dynamite, they use black powder," Christopher said.

"Which is one bad idea," Rudy said, "since black powder burns when it blows. Starts more fires than it stops."

Two more booms echoed in the distance.

Cousin Judith threw up her hands. "All I know is that we're going to get these people moved into the house. I've decided that any more aftershocks won't be strong enough to bother us."

"We'd better get to work clearing out some of the plaster and debris then," Albert said, "and hope that you're right about those aftershocks."

The next several hours were spent in ceaseless work as everyone pitched in to clean space for the refugees in the front hall and parlor and dining room of the house. As soon as the injured and their families were safely moved, there were other jobs to be done. The men moved the cookstove to the backyard for better cooking. A soldier had told them Wednesday night that cooking indoors was forbidden in the city until further notice.

Holly and Caroline took charge of the soup kettle that had to be kept simmering all the time. With so many to feed, the girls chopped vegetables and stirred for hours. When they had a spare moment, it was spent washing cups and bowls.

Mark and Curtis and Clifford carried endless buckets of water and kettles of soup. The three women cared for the injured and comforted everyone. Mark often saw his mother holding someone's hand with head bowed, obviously praying.

By noon it was apparent to Mark that the fires still roared westward. The orange flames looked much closer and more menacing. Mark couldn't keep from going back to the front curb every so often to stare eastward. It was hard to understand why God allowed such a terrifying monster to continue its march. Had He deserted them, deserted everyone in this city? But why, Mark kept asking. Why?

CHAPTER 13

Time to Go

"We won't stay if we're not needed, and we'll be back as soon as possible," Albert said when the three men and Clifford left to go again to the fire line shortly before one o'clock.

The flood of refugees past the Dunlap home had ebbed, making it possible for the women to care for those in the house with only the younger cousins to help. Some of the less seriously injured refugees had already resumed their trek west to the Presidio.

"We have to help if we can," Christopher said to Mother.

"If the fire can't be stopped at Van Ness Avenue, the whole west side of the city will burn," Albert said grimly. "The fire won't stop until it burns to the ocean."

"Go," Mother said with a sigh, "but please be careful.

Let's also take a moment to pray before you leave."

Everyone gathered on the front porch of the Dunlap house and bowed their heads as Mother prayed for safety. A frightening image of the fire at the ocean flashed through Mark's head. How could the flames travel so far? It was miles from the Dunlaps' house to the beach, where Mark had collected shells on Monday. "Please, God, please," he whispered, "help."

Mark watched from the curb until the four figures disappeared from sight.

Mother put her arm on Mark's shoulder. "God will be with them," she said.

"Why did God make this earthquake happen?" Mark asked. "Was he punishing San Francisco?"

"Some people would say that," Mother conceded, "but I don't think that's the case. God lets nature take its course in this world. That includes earthquakes and fires. He wants us to trust in Him even in the middle of terrible times."

"We've prayed, and I bet lots of other people have prayed that the fires would stop, but they haven't. Maybe it will get worse. Why doesn't God listen?"

"Oh, He listens." Mother reached out to push Mark's hair back. "God always listens to us, and He always answers our prayers. Trouble is, the answers sometimes aren't the ones we want. He may say yes to our prayers, or no, or wait awhile. I think the wait awhile answer is the hardest one. I don't like to wait, and I know you don't."

"Will God keep Christopher and the others safe?"

"I think so, and I know that He'll be right there beside them, lending strength and helping them figure things out." Mother hugged Mark close. "Come on, let's get back to work. No doubt someone in there needs something."

Mark took a deep breath of the smoky air and followed Mother back into the house. He went right to the water buckets. It seemed like they were always empty. It was probably an hour later that he went out front again with Curtis.

When he looked east, he saw specks of something in the air. "What's blowing in the wind?"

Curtis frowned and stepped over to where a small chunk had landed on the ground.

"It's a cinder, isn't it?" Mark asked.

"Afraid so," Curtis replied. "It's burned out, but that's what it is."

"If we start getting live cinders, they could start fires here."

"I guess so," Curtis said.

"What do we do?" Mark asked. Now that he knew what they were, he could see thousands of tiny cinders swirling through the air above them.

"I don't know that there is anything we can do but leave if the fires start."

"We'd have to take these people with us," Mark said. "How would we do that? Some of them can't walk."

"We need a wagon or an automobile or something."

"What about that friend of your family?" Mark asked. "The ones that took Mrs. Temple to the country."

"Mr. Jackson?"

"Yes, what about his auto? He said it was trapped in the shed. Maybe we could get it out." Just then Mark heard another series of explosions. They seemed closer.

"We could try," Curtis said. "But who would drive it?

Nobody left around here knows how to drive."

"I can drive," Mark said. "Uncle Abe taught me. Come on, let's go ask your mother." They went inside and told their idea to Cousin Judith and Mother.

The two women came outside long enough to look at the cinders in the air and the fire line that showed no sign of stopping.

"We may have to leave," Cousin Judith said quietly. "We'd best make plans."

"I hope the men will be back soon," Mother said, "but we can't wait for that."

"See what you can do about the automobile, boys, if Polly is willing," Cousin Judith said and looked at Mother, who nodded. "William would want us to use it, I'm sure. We'll get these people ready to move."

"Be careful, Mark," Mother said and gave him a quick kiss.

The boys raced down the street and behind the Jacksons' house. A big oak tree had split in the earthquake with half of it falling across the wide door to the shed. They looked at the tree from all angles.

"I think we can get the auto out, barely, if we get rid of that one limb," Mark said. "Maybe there's a saw of some sort in the shed."

"We'll find out soon enough," Curtis said and ducked under the tree limbs to get in the shed. Moments later he emerged grinning, with saw in hand.

The boys took turns sawing at the limb until it dropped at their feet. They tugged and pulled at it until a narrow path was cleared for the auto. Mark climbed into the vehicle's seat and studied the knobs and switches. Not much different from Uncle Abe's auto. He jumped out to show Curtis how to crank, and then he hopped back into the driver's seat. He closed his eyes for a second before waving for Curtis to crank. *Please, God, let this auto start.*

When Curtis cranked, the engine sputtered twice and then caught. Mark adjusted the throttle until the engine ran smoothly. He eased the auto into gear and slowly backed out of the shed.

Curtis stood back a little, wide-eyed. "You really can drive."

"I can, and you'd better hop in if you want a ride home." Mark reached over and swung open the passenger side door.

Curtis didn't hesitate but scrambled into the auto. The automobile chugged down the street toward home. Mark made a wide U-turn in the street and parked in front of the Dunlap house.

Mother and Cousin Judith came running out with Holly and Caroline close behind. Bernetta peered out the door as well.

"You did it," Mother said proudly.

"So now we have it, if we have to get out fast," Cousin Judith said. "Which may be any time."

The cinders still floated down, but now some of them glowed red briefly before vanishing. Mark realized that rather than being stopped, the fire must have roared closer during the hour it took them to free the car.

"Mother," someone called from down the street. Clifford darted among the few people who still traveled westward. A young man in an army uniform was right behind him.

"Where's your father and the others?" Cousin Judith asked as soon as Clifford skidded to a stop in front of her.

"Are you all right?" Clifford's face was streaked with dirt and sweat, as were his clothes.

"I'm fine. We got separated," Clifford said. "The fire is just on the east side of Van Ness Avenue. We were laying fire hose. Sometimes there's a little water from a hydrant. I got cut off from them, so I came back here. I met my friend George's older brother Samuel on the way. He's in the army and going to the Presidio. He's supposed to help out there, but it will also give him an opportunity to check on his father."

Samuel nodded at Cousin Judith. "Clifford tells me that you have injured in your house. If so, they need to be moved right away. The fire could jump Van Ness at any time. It may have already jumped in fact."

"We were just talking about that," Cousin Judith said. "Mark and Curtis have provided us with this fine vehicle, so I think we'd better start moving our guests to the Presidio now. How is your father doing? We were concerned when we learned about the accident yesterday."

"He's holding his own, ma'am. Thank you for your concern," Samuel said. "And now we'd better tend to your injured here."

Within a few minutes two of the more seriously injured refugees had been loaded into the auto. With a wide board placed across the back seat, two people could lie down. Bernetta would go along as well as Caroline and Holly. Bernetta's nursing ability would make her valuable at the hospital. The girls could help her and, more importantly, be out of the way of the fire.

The girls and Bernetta crowded into the front seat, while Samuel and Curtis rode on the running boards, clinging to the sides of the auto.

"We'll get the others ready," Mother called to Mark as the auto moved slowly into the middle of the street. "Clifford will help us get them to the curb. They'll be there when you get back."

The trip to the Presidio didn't take long, even though Mark drove slowly. At the gates, a soldier ran in front of the auto, hands out.

"Hail there," he yelled. "By whose authority are you driving that automobile? The military has commandeered all autos for relief work."

Samuel jumped down from the running board and walked up to the soldier. "This is relief work, Corporal, and I am a member of the military."

The corporal saluted briskly. "Sorry, sir, I didn't see you."

"We'll be taking these injured civilians to the hospital and then the boys will be going back for another load. If that meets with your approval."

"Yes, sir, but Captain, I'd suggest that you get a pass for them. It's not safe without one."

"Good idea, Corporal," Samuel said. "I'll see to that."

In ten minutes, Mark and Curtis had unloaded everyone, obtained an official pass, and were on their way back to the house. Samuel had gone to look for his injured father, while Caroline and Holly were helping Bernetta get their charges settled in the hospital.

The two boys made five more trips over the next two hours, and still the fire showed no signs of slowing. Christopher and the others hadn't returned, and the cinders had become burning chunks that were falling everywhere. Mark heard the distant roaring and crackling of the flames as they devoured everything in their path. Darkness descended quickly since the light was already dimmed by the smoke. Mark stood on the curb one last time and stared eastward. The whole eastern sky glowed orange. Every now and then a boom would echo.

"Mark, we have to go," Mother said quietly. "The last of the refugees are loaded. Judith left a note on the door. Christopher and Albert and Rudy will find us at the Presidio. There's nothing else we can do here."

Mark wrenched his eyes away from the fire that almost seemed alive to him now. He squeezed into the crowded auto with Mother, Cousin Judith, and the last two injured men, while Clifford and Curtis clung to the running board. The Dunlaps' dog, Captain, trotted obediently alongside. Without another look back, Mark drove them to safety.

They had barely unloaded at the Presidio when an older man walked up and demanded to know whose automobile they had arrived in.

"Ours, sort of," Curtis said. He and Mark had been left with the auto while Clifford helped Cousin Judith and Mother get the injured men inside the hospital.

"Where's the driver?" The uniformed man looked around.

"Right here," Mark said and pointed to himself.

"You, the driver!" The man snorted his disbelief. "You're just a boy."

"He's been driving for hours while we brought some injured people to the hospital," Curtis said indignantly.

"Well, I can't use a boy," the man said and yanked his head around. "Sergeant," he bellowed. Another uniformed man came running from the side of a nearby building. "Did you find a driver? I found an automobile."

"No, sir. There are no drivers left."

"We've got to find someone. Those boxes have to get to the fire line." He pointed to two wooden crates sitting on the grass. "Are you sure you can't drive, Sergeant Ames?"

"I'm sure, Captain Cooper." The sergeant backed up a step. "I've never put my hand to a car even once, sir."

"Begging your pardon, sir." Another voice said from behind Mark. It was the corporal from the gate. "This here boy can drive just fine."

Captain Cooper frowned and looked around once more. Throwing up his hands he said, "Guess he'll have to do. Hop to, boy. This is a desperate situation."

"I don't know that he should go," Curtis said.

"None of us should go there, son," Captain Cooper said, "but this city is about to burn to the sea. These supplies may help."

"I'll go," Mark said. "Tell Mother I'll be back as soon as I can. I have to help."

Curtis looked frightened, but he nodded. "I'll tell her." He moved over to crank the auto for Mark.

The sergeant loaded the crates and climbed in the back seat while the captain got in front with Mark. In a moment Mark waved to Curtis, and they were off with their cargo. The street was nearly clear of traffic. Mark switched on the headlights and could see the cinders. They looked like fiery snowflakes.

Captain Cooper directed Mark to drive to Lafayette Park. Once there, they all climbed out and joined hundreds of other people crowded onto the highest hill. The captain peered through a pair of binoculars down at the fire. Mark assumed that he was searching for the place to deliver the supplies.

Mark was awed by the horrible panorama before him. The flames made a complete semicircle around the eastern side of the city. A cloud of flame swooped down like a bird on a section of buildings on a hill across Van Ness. The buildings were engulfed in fire instantly. He heard the boom of dynamite and saw an upshot of burning timbers and sparks. Once in awhile he saw figures and assumed they were firefighters. He hoped that Christopher and the others had retreated safely.

"Let's go, boy," Captain Cooper barked. "I see where the command post is. We'll drop off this dynamite and high-tail it back to the Presidio."

"Dynamite!" Mark said. "I didn't know this was dynamite." He climbed back in the auto and looked warily in the back seat at the crates.

"It's the last we have until a new supply arrives." Captain Cooper shook his head. "I just hope this is enough."

In minutes they were so close to the fire that Mark could feel the heat. The captain directed him to drive down Gough Street to Pine. The fire raged only a block or so east. Everywhere soldiers and firemen and policemen raced back and forth with hoses and shovels and buckets.

Finally Captain Cooper ordered Mark to stop. He ordered the sergeant to unload the crates. In a few moments some other soldiers, supervised by Captain Cooper, carried the crates toward Van Ness. Mark looked toward the fire down Pine Street and saw a big gun sitting with its barrel pointed east. "Is that a cannon?" he asked a fireman who had stopped to fix his boot.

"Sure thing," the fireman said. "They brought in the artillery earlier to blow up some of the houses on the east side of Van Ness. They stopped shelling here because the fire's too close now for it to do any good." The fireman stood up and looked more closely at Mark. "Say, boy, you'd better get out of here. This line could go any time."

"I have to wait on Captain Cooper and the sergeant. I'm their driver."

The fireman shrugged and picked up his shovel. "Recruiting them awful young these days. At least get farther back."

Mark wasn't sure what to do. He didn't want to leave the two soldiers, but they were nowhere in sight. At last he climbed into the still running auto and drove a block west. He parked and ran back toward the fire to find the captain and sergeant.

Cinders flew through the air, which felt like an oven had been flung open. As Mark ran, a cinder landed on a patch of dry grass and ignited a tiny fire. He grabbed a wet sack that lay in the middle of the street and quickly extinguished the flames. All the time he yelled for the captain, but there was no sign of him or the sergeant. Mark had decided to turn back to the auto when shouts rose over the roar of the fire a block away.

"It's across! It's across!" The words echoed down the street as men took up the cry. "It's across at Sacramento." Mark stopped. The fire had done what they had worked for hours to prevent. It had jumped wide Van Ness Avenue, which was supposed to halt it. Now there was no stopping the flames before the Pacific Ocean. The city was lost.

CHAPTER 14
Rescue

Mark stood where he was for several moments, his mind a jumble of conflicting thoughts. The fire was coming directly at him, but he didn't want to leave Captain Cooper and the sergeant. Besides, he wasn't sure that he knew how to get back to the Presidio on his own. And what about Christopher and Rudy and Albert? Where were they? Did they need help?

As he retreated a few steps toward the auto, two soldiers trotted past him. "Have you seen Captain Cooper?" he yelled.

"Don't know him," one answered.

"Unless he's that grouchy one with the dynamite," the other one said.

"That's him. Which way did he go?" Mark asked.

"That way," the first soldier said and pointed north. "Toward Sacramento Street."

"Thanks!" Mark shouted as the two men disappeared from sight in the smoke.

Mark made a quick decision. He'd drive the car north a couple blocks, park, and take a quick look east up Sacramento Street toward the fire. If he didn't find the captain there, he'd get in the auto and find his own way back to the Presidio.

He was surprised to find that the fire wasn't raging along Sacramento Street the way it was on the east side of Van Ness. At least not yet. Several houses were on fire, but they hadn't yet formed a wall of flames. Even so, the cinders and hot wind swirled around him as he ran toward the fire line and then cut back to go parallel to it. He still carried the wet sack and occasionally stopped to beat out tiny fires that licked the grass along the street.

Firemen and soldiers and other men did the same as Mark. They smothered the tiny flames, but the big fire hoses lay limp and empty. Mark saw only one hose working, and as he watched, it, too, sputtered and ran dry. Still there was no sign of Captain Cooper, and the fires were starting to gather strength.

A flurry of activity drew Mark's attention just as he had decided to give up his search. Two men with a fireman rushed by and stopped at a fire hydrant.

"We can't quit now," one of them yelled. "One of these hydrants will surely have some water." The fireman leaned over the hydrant with a tool while the others watched. He turned the tool. Suddenly water gushed out of the hydrant opening.

A cheer rang out from the group. The fireman quickly

twisted the hydrant closed and ran for a hose.

"You were right," another man said. "It took seven hydrants, but you found one."

They grabbed the hose from the fireman and wrestled it into place at the hydrant. Mark moved closer. One of those men had a familiar look from the back. His eyes felt so gritty with cinders and smoke that he wasn't sure if he could trust what he thought he saw. Then the man turned as he yanked at the hose.

"Christopher!" Mark yelled. His stepfather straightened up and turned. His face was black, and his eyes were red from the smoke, but his white teeth still shone as he smiled when he recognized Mark.

"Mark! What in the world? How did you get here? Is everyone safe?" Christopher reached for Mark and crushed him in a fierce hug.

"I'm fine," Mark said. "It's a long story how I got here, but the rest of the family is fine. They're at the Presidio."

"What about Clifford? We got separated from him."

"He's there, too."

"We've got to get you out of here," Christopher said. He looked around.

A chorus of cheers interrupted him as the fire hose stiffened with the weight of the water. A hundred feet from the hydrant the nozzle sprayed a steady stream of water on the flames.

"Help us here, would you?" another fireman yelled as he struggled to move the heavy hose closer.

Christopher jumped to help, and Mark tugged the hose alongside him. In seconds they were close enough to hear the hissing as the water hit the flames. Other men pulled pumpers and more hose from farther down the street.

They fought the fire in two directions. One set of hoses rained water on the buildings that crackled with fire on the east side of the street. The other set doused the houses not yet on fire on the west side. Firemen swarmed over those buildings, trying to put out each small blaze before it could take hold.

Mark and Christopher pulled hose until Mark's shoulders ached. Over their head flew water and cinders and always smoke, choking smoke. Mark's nose and throat burned each time he took a breath.

They pulled hose to one more house that had only a small blaze on the lower part of its roof. A fireman was climbing the roof to get a better angle for the hose when he lost his balance. In a flash he was falling, desperately clawing for a handhold across the steep roof. Christopher was closest and ran forward as if to stop his fall. The fireman caught hold of the edge of the roof for a moment and then fell. Christopher reached up at the same time, and they both dropped to the ground when the fireman tumbled down.

"Christopher!" Mark screamed. He reached his stepfather in moments. Christopher lay crumpled and still. The fireman rolled over and sat up.

Gently Mark touched Christopher's face. "Wake up! Please God, let him wake up." In a second his stepfather's eyelids fluttered open.

"Ouch," he said softly, but grinned at Mark, who leaned close.

"Are you all right?"

"I think so, all things considered," Christopher said.

"You broke my fall," the fireman said. "Probably saved

my life. Are you sure you're all right?"

"I'm fine. Just let me get up." Christopher took Mark's hand and pulled himself up a foot only to plop down again. "My side hurts," he said through gritted teeth.

"What's wrong?" Mark asked.

"I don't know, maybe broken ribs," Christopher said and wrapped his arms around his middle. "Can you help me get out of the way?"

"Sure, can you put your arm on my shoulder?" Mark asked. Gingerly he helped his stepfather up.

"My ankle doesn't feel so hot either," Christopher said and winced when he tried to take a step. "Let me rest for a minute, and then we'll get out of here."

Just then someone yelled to the fireman. Christopher told the man he was fine, and the fireman limped quickly down the street to the pumper.

"Let's go," Mark said. "The water might give out at any time. I saw it happen earlier." He helped Christopher walk, but the man gasped with pain with each step. It was soon obvious that his stepfather couldn't go much farther. The flames were terrifyingly close, and Mark knew that he could never carry or even drag Christopher to safety.

They made it a block, but then Mark steered Christopher over to the curb.

"You wait here," Mark ordered. "I'll go after the auto."

"Auto," Christopher wheezed. "What auto?"

"Another long story. Don't move. I'll be right back."

Mark flew down the street to find the automobile right where he had left it. Mark drove as fast as he dared up Sacramento Street and circled widely, pulling up right in front of Christopher.

"What service," Christopher croaked weakly.

Mark helped his stepfather in the front seat, and soon they fairly flew north. "What happened to Rudy and Albert?"

"We were going to meet at the house if we got separated."

"Cousin Judith left a note on the door when we left."

"Good, that means that we can go right on to the Presidio." Christopher leaned his head back against the seat.

Mark glanced at his stepfather from time to time as he drove through the dark streets. Christopher's face was white where the black grime didn't cover it. Was he hurt somewhere inside, something worse than a broken rib or ankle? All Mark could do was drive as fast as he dared.

The Presidio gate loomed ahead and was a welcome sight to Mark. He zoomed past the same corporal who had been on duty earlier and gently braked to a stop in front of the hospital. He ran inside and returned with two orderlies and a stretcher. In no time, Christopher was carried away down a long hall. Mark was left to worry on a bench in a waiting room. He wanted to look for his mother but was afraid to leave in case Christopher needed him.

An hour passed with no word. Mark sat with bowed head, praying for all he was worth. He didn't think he could bear to lose someone else.

"Mark! Oh, Mark! Are you all right?" Mother swooped down on him and hugged him so tight he thought he'd break. After she finished, Holly grabbed him. Mark saw that the rest of the family was right behind them, including Albert and Rudy.

"I'm fine," Mark answered at last. "But Christopher, he's hurt. I'm not sure how bad."

"He'll be fine, love," Mother said. "We found him first.

139

We didn't know you were out here until we talked to him. He has broken ribs, which are painful, but not life threatening. Luckily they didn't puncture his lungs, which are already irritated from all that smoke. The doctor also thinks his ankle is just badly sprained rather than broken. He'll be good as new in a couple weeks."

"I'm glad," Mark said. Relief poured over him like a warm river.

"I was frightened out of my wits for you," Mother said severely. "When Curtis told us what had happened, I thought I'd faint. The idea of that captain making a boy drive for him."

"They needed me," Mark said.

"I know, but that doesn't make me like it," Mother said. "What supplies could possibly have been so vital that they ordered a twelve-year-old boy to drive?"

Mark gulped. "Actually, it was dynamite. But I didn't know that," he said quickly as his mother's jaw dropped.

"Well, I never," she sputtered. "I'll be having a word or two with that captain if I can find him."

Privately Mark hoped that Captain Cooper stayed safely away from Mother. "Where is Christopher?"

"He's in a bed in the hallway, but he'll be able to leave in the morning," said Cousin Judith.

"If we have any place to go to," Caroline said.

"Now, we won't think like that," Cousin Judith said. "God has kept us safe with no serious injuries. We can deal with anything else. Tonight we'll camp here in the Presidio, and tomorrow we'll go home."

"I'm right proud of you, lad," Rudy said and put his hand on Mark's shoulder. "I've got a feeling you've got quite a story to tell."

Mark nodded at the cowboy and grinned.

"Let's go check on Christopher," Mother said. They all traipsed down the long hall past dozens of injured who rested in beds and cots crowded into every inch of space.

Christopher lay on a cot at the very end of the hallway. His face looked white, and Mark realized that someone had made an attempt to wash the soot and sweat off. Christopher grinned weakly at the group.

Mark felt suddenly shy. He was so glad that Christopher was going to get well, but it seemed impossible to voice that.

"Thanks, Mark. I don't know what I would have done without you," Christopher said. He put his good arm out and pulled Mark closer. "My son is brave and incredibly resourceful and quite the speedy driver."

Everyone laughed, which gave Mark a moment to take a deep breath.

"I'm just happy that you two are in one piece," Mother said, "but speaking of sons, we've got to get a message to Peter and the girls that this branch of the family is banged up but safe."

Mark looked down at Christopher and then at Mother and Holly, who had squeezed onto the edge of Christopher's cot. Were they a family now? Could he bear to think of them that way? The answer came to him with a surge of joy. Yes, he could. It wasn't the same family as before, with his father, but it was a family all the same.

"The wind has turned!" someone yelled down the hall. "It should turn the fire, too."

Mark and Curtis ran out a nearby door. They dashed to the top of a small rise in front of the hospital. The glow of the fire was distant, but it still filled the eastern sky. The wind blew strongly from the west, from the ocean. Mark felt it on his neck. It should force the fire back toward the burned-out area. There was a chance, a good chance, that the west side of the city was saved.

Mark looked up into the sky. The brisk wind had stirred the smoky air until a single star winked through a gap in the haze. Maybe it was the same star that Mark had noticed just two nights ago on the way home from the Caruso performance. It hadn't changed. He had and San Francisco had, but not the star. And he could trust that star to still be there tomorrow, no matter what. Just like God could be trusted to always be there.

Mark sucked in a deep breath of air that now smelled as strongly of salt from the ocean as it had smelled of smoke an hour ago. "I have to say, Curtis, that in spite of all the excitement, I'm starved. Let's see if any of these soldiers have a pot of soup cooking."

Curtis laughed, and the two cousins headed back into the hospital, arms around each other's shoulders.

By the next morning, Mark and the others knew that the fire had definitely turned back on itself when the wind changed directions. The Dunlap home was spared, but the fire roared across the northeast part of San Francisco for almost another whole day before finally dying on Friday night.

Mark and Curtis and their families, along with the dog, returned to the Dunlap house on Saturday morning. Rudy and Bernetta said good-bye and traveled south to Bernetta's home in San Jose. Like thousands of other families, the Dunlaps faced weeks of cleanup. Margarite showed up two days later to help. Her family was safe and living with other relatives.

Christopher was healing quickly and already was able to type as he spent hours recording events of the quake for the newspaper.

Albert sent a telegram to Peter and the girls on Saturday when he went to see what was left of his bank. It was a burned-out shell, but Albert told Mark that they'd needed more room anyway.

Mark and Holly and Mother helped sweep up and cart out debris from the house. They slept inside but cooked outdoors since the ban on indoor fires was still in effect. As soon as Christopher was sufficiently healed, the family would head back to Minneapolis.

As much as Mark had liked San Francisco, he was ready to go home. He couldn't wait to tell Maureen and Jens about all his adventures. He was also ready to give Christopher another chance. Mark might not need a new father, but he did need an older and wiser friend. He had a feeling that Christopher might become just that.

There's More!

The American Adventure continues in *Marching with Sousa*. When Mark and Holly return from San Francisco, Mark's best friend, Jens, stops speaking to him. Holly's friends are jealous of her, and Mark and Holly's stepfather doesn't seem to have any time for his family.

Mark must choose between doing what his mother and band teacher want him to do or keeping his friendship with Jens. Holly must choose between being best friends with Camille or being friends with the other girls in her class.

When the time comes to take action, will Mark and Holly find a way to make things right?